It was not until ~~she reached the~~ door of her room that she looked over her shoulder. Before she could cry out, Retaux lunged from the shadows and grabbed her arm. Just as quickly, Jeanne's hand whipped into her reticule to pull out a small pistol and thrust it against his cheek.

Retaux blinked; Jeanne cocked the glittering little gun, forcing him back against the rail on the landing. The rotted wood creaked dangerously, bending beneath his weight as Retaux craned his neck to stare two floors down.

"You inserted yourself into this situation, Monsieur," Jeanne hissed. "How do you propose to take leave of it?"

"Ahh." Retaux cleared his throat delicately, then whispered, "Have you any suggestions?"

"Find use for yourself on my behalf." The pistol's mouth bored into his cheek. "Quickly."

Behind him the railing quivered. Its creak became a groan, as the posts began to give way.

"Madame!" Retaux blurted desperately. "At court the trick to obtaining your desires is to first know what everyone else desires!"

"Yes?" Jeanne regarded him coolly. "And you have such knowledge?"

Retaux smiled nervously. "It is my second greatest talent."

Jeanne's face softened slightly. Retaux's smile grew broader and more confident; he lifted a hand to move the gun away.

"*Non.*" The gun jabbed even harder against his cheek. "Make no mistake, Monsieur. I hold the power between us."

The Affair of the Necklace

A Novelization by ELIZABETH HAND

Based on the Screenplay by JOHN SWEET

HarperEntertainment
An Imprint of HarperCollinsPublishers

ALCON
ENTERTAINMENT

HarperEntertainment
An Imprint of HarperCollins*Publishers*
10 East 53rd Street
New York, NY 10022-5299

ISBN: 0-06-107616-3

First HarperEntertainment paperback printing: September 2001

Printed in the United States of America

Visit HarperEntertainment on the World Wide Web at
www.harpercollins.com

10   9   8   7   6   5   4   3

Napoleon wrote that the French Revolution was the result of three factors:

The defeat at Rosbach during the Seven Years' War; lack of intervention in the Dutch Netherlands; and *L'Affaire du Collier*—the Affair of the Necklace.

The following is inspired by a true story.

PROLOGUE

I have dread revelations to make as my time grows short. You may wonder that I speak of such things now, but I assure you that it is far easier to sing out my sorrows like a lonely nightingale, than to suffer in dark silence. And so I will answer the question that I know each of you holds within your heart, imprisoned as so many of us have been imprisoned during these dark days —

How was it that my name became so disastrously linked with that of a great queen, and of a prince clad in the purple and gold vestments of the Roman Church? And why is it that I, the Comtesse de La

Motte, born Jeanne Valois, must pay for their sins as well as my own?

How did it come to this, you ask; and now I will tell you.

The name. It all goes back to the name.

Chapter

O N E

❧

I was born twenty-eight years ago of illustrious origin. Royal blood flows in my veins: retrace five generations and you come upon a king. Some of you might not have believed this, seeing the girl I was—once upon a time, as Monsieur Perrault might have said in one of his tales for a winter's night. And yet I tell you it is true: as real as if you were to take your fingernail and draw it, hard, across the cheek of a painted wanton, and see the blood seep out from beneath the veneer of white lead and rouge that she wears.

The truth of my name is that blood. It courses through me, hot and never still; in my darkest hours it casts a glow upon my thoughts. It is, simply, what keeps me alive.

Sadly for me, in the year that my tale starts, the Valois name had fallen upon difficult times. Through no fault of our own, unless one can say that the innocent who walks down a street only to be beset by brigands is to be blamed for the theft of his gold. But I will tell you, the loss of one's purse is as nothing as to the loss of one's home; and even that pales before the loss of one's name.

Until I was eight years old, I lived in a kingdom of gold. These riches came not from our holdings, which were extensive but not excessive—a three-storied château surrounded by miles of oak forest and swelling hills and fields where rye grew, and summer wheat, and apples so sweet that each autumn you would cry out with joy when first you bit into one. No, the riches which nourished me were those that came from seeing, each day, the faces of my parents drawn close together over the table at breakfast: their laughter and delight in each other, and in me, their only child. My mother, Irene, was twenty-seven years old, a gentle but intelligent woman. She painted, for her pleasure and that of my father, Darnell, who proudly hung her work alongside portraits of our ancestors in the grand but chilly formal rooms of our home. She read to me as well. Not just Perrault's stories and *les contes de ma Mére l'Oie*, the tales of Mother Goose which every child hears, but also the fairy tales of Voltaire, as well as his *Candide*, and the amusing plays of Molière, of which my father was especially fond. But my favorite of all these was *"Le Chat botté,"* Puss in Boots, the tale of the brave and clever cat who comes to the aid of his owner, a young boy who has been disinherited by evil men. My mother used to laugh as I dressed myself in the gardener's cast-off shoes to stomp around the bedroom, acting out for her brave Puss's adventures, and ending of course with honor and the family fortunes restored. As she entered the last days of her confinement with her second child, my darling baby sister, I would turn from my bloodthirsty dramas to the calmer stage of our garden. There I would swing while my mother painted, and my father saw to all the responsibilities of running an estate.

Perhaps because my mother was painting me that day—I remember vividly peering over her shoulder at the little canvas—I can still recall exactly how it happened. My father had come up to see us, his boots still dusted with black earth and gold straw from where he had been overseeing the harvest. He too stopped to observe the progress of my mother's painting, and to check as well the progress of their joint creative effort, the child swelling in her womb. His hand caressed her belly straining against her silk skirt: I can see the two of them now, as clearly as though they were on a painted canvas in front of me. Nothing and no one has ever seemed as lovely to me as they were then.

I knew that I belonged with them, and to them, Irene and Darnell Valois. That knowledge was what made me rich, that knowledge was my birthright; and so I launched myself from the swing to tumble laughing at their feet, my skirts flung up over my head and my parents laughing as I shook the folds of fabric from my face and gazed up at them, as happy as I had ever been. As happy as I would ever be.

"Grace in all its form and glory," my mother laughed.

"Jeanne!" my father called, his tone mock accusing. "Have you forgotten? You promised to take me for a ride today."

"I have not forgotten!" I cried, running into his arms. He kissed my mother good-bye, tenderly; then, sweeping me up alongside him, headed for the stables.

We galloped across the fields that lay to the west of our home. Ring-necked doves flew up from the long grass, crying plaintively, and little yellow butterflies like a swarm of golden coins falling upward instead of down. I sat on the saddle in front of my father, his right hand holding tight to the reins, his left arm locked around me. It was the safest place in all the world; and from that vantage point I saw all the rest of the world as part of that domain, a kingdom in which I had nothing to fear. We rode up the ridge, to a clearing from whence we could see all the way across the valley to where the river ran like mercury through emerald glass. Here my father reined his horse in, calming it with a few low words. I turned in the saddle to gaze up at him, his eyes catching the sun and glowing as he gazed down at me. He kissed the tip of his finger, touched it to my nose, and whispered, "*Je t'aime*, Jeanne."

"*Je t'aime*, Papa."

But before I could reach to embrace him, his gaze sharpened. He straightened in the saddle, turning and frowning slightly. All the warmth in his face faded.

"What is this, then?" he murmured.

I turned as well. Down the narrow winding road that led to our estate, two dozen men on horseback were galloping. They were armed. As I watched, they swerved from the road and began thundering up the path toward the ridge where my father and I waited. The late afternoon light glanced from their helmets, and as they drew nearer I saw that they carried pikes, each one sharp and dazzling as a razor. My father's big hand circled my arm, holding me tight; and though I knew I was not as strong my own small hand rested atop his. In this way I tried to give him comfort; to let him know, like the brave *Chat botté*, that I would do everything in my power to defend our name.

I was a child. I did not know, then, that brave cats and benevolent fairy grandmothers are only the stuff of wonder tales. I was very soon to learn.

Chapter

T W O

❧❧

Duc d'Amar, a distant cousin of the reigning Bourbons, had long coveted my father's land. Eager to expand his holdings, the Duke convinced King Louis XV to issue a letter of cachet. This dreaded document allowed our lands—all of the Valois holdings—to be seized without cause by d'Amar. It was the Duke's soldiers who appeared that afternoon, a swarm of filthy rats despoiling and devouring the golden fields and sunlit rooms of my childhood. It was d'Amar's men who dragged the chairs and tables from our dining room into the courtyard, and there set them ablaze, along with the feather mattress from my own room and the beautifully carved bassinet that had been passed down in our family for five generations; the bassinet was intended to hold my dear baby sister when she was born. And it was the Duke d'Amar's men who beat my father, twenty cowards against one brave man; beat him until he fell unconscious onto the cobblestones before the bonfire they had made of my world; beat him and shackled him and threw him into the back of a flatbed wagon, as though he were a sack of rye to be brought to market; as though he were already dead.

I screamed as they drove away, running after the wagon as it rattled through the courtyard and out into the darkness. I never saw my father again. He was locked up at the pleasure of His Majesty, Louis XV, the man some called the Beloved but whom I knew now and ever after to be a brute. I learned later that he died in the Bastille, a victim of the inhumane horrors that awaited those who lacked the favor of the King.

My mother's fate was no less tragic. Shortly after my father was taken by d'Amar's men, my mother gave birth to my sister. Not in the warmth and light of her own château, as should have happened, attended by midwives and loving family; but on filthy straw in a hovel outside the neighboring village. She died the next morning. There was no attending physician to declare the cause of death as childbed fever, indeed there was no one there at all save myself and an elderly woman servant who had refused to leave my mother's side. And at any rate I knew my mother did not die of fever. She died of heart-break and despair, as deadly as the pox or the plague in those days, and as fatal.

And so it was that I became my sister's keeper. The kindly servant found us a wet-nurse, a woman from the village whose own child had died. My sister lived, but she did not thrive. There were those who took pity upon us, but there were just as many who were unwilling, or simply unable to share the little they had with two orphans. To help sustain us, I relied on the only asset that remained: our heritage.

I blush now, not with shame but sorrow, to recall my child-self in rags, my baby sister, *ma petite ange*, bundled upon my back as I went from town to town. One could always find a fire blazing outside the village inn, warming carriage-drivers and itinerants and sometimes the merely curious, who would stop to hold their hands before the flames and exchange news and gossip. I learned to approach with my head held up — beggars might be stoned, or kicked — and my voice strong as I called out to them.

"We are orphaned children who descend in a direct line from Henri II, one of our country's greatest kings. Any kindness bestowed upon us now will be remembered when we resume our proper place in the world."

I would smile then, disarmingly, and hold out my hand: not like a beggar, but as one who greets a friend. Sometimes we would meet with generosity and kindness. More often, the travelers would jeer at us and laugh, bowing and scraping in mock homage, dusting the ground with their hats and then shaking the dust in my face. I would only gaze at them, pride and nobility still evident in my demeanor if not my clothes. It is astonishing how often the good peasants failed to recognize royalty.

Our former servants showed unquestionable kindness to *mon ange* and myself, giving us shelter and sharing the few crumbs they had. We would huddle together on a straw pallet, my poor wee sister thin as a straw herself; I would try to warm her against my breast, and to amuse her I showed her the few things I had managed to save from d'Amar's rats. A locket with my mother's cameo inside; a small enameled box. This last was my most treasured possession, not because of its gilt engraving but because of what it held: the only surviving copy of the Valois genealogy chart, as worn and frayed as a map of ancient times. There were gilt lilies within the shield of the family crest, and *mon ange*'s tiny hand would reach for these, as though she knew what they portended and strove to seize her birthright for herself.

But nothing could quell the pain of having so much taken away so swiftly. How could it ever be made right again? I would take my baby sister's hand, and in the cold and frigid darkness whisper to her.

"Some day we will be ladies and wear fine clothes. Our house will be the grandest for miles around. We will have parties, and be surrounded by people who love us. Father will come back so we can be a family again. Just the way it was."

And I would kiss her finger and touch it to the tip of her nose, just as Father did to me.

Chapter

THREE

~❧❦~

It was on an unpromising winter morning that our lives changed. I had made it my job to treat each day as though it were a gift, a package finely or crudely wrapped but a gift all the same, with who knows what inside. This particular morning, however, the package seemed to have been thrown into the mud then trodden into slush by the hooves of passing horses.

Or so it felt to me, anyway, standing outside, shivering as the first cold hard flakes fell from a sky the color of a scorched pan. My little sister was, as always, bundled upon my back. There had been nothing for me to eat that morning, though I had hopes of later finding a potato, or perhaps a few leaves of winter kale, dropped from a passing farmer's wagon—that was what had brought me to this particular thoroughfare. My sister's first teeth were breaking through, and she had kept me up most of the night before, whimpering or wailing with pain. Now I thrust my hand back over my shoulder, so that she could teethe upon my knuckle, still raw from last night.

"There, there," I murmured, bouncing up and down to distract her. "Who's my good girl? Who's—"

From down the muddy road echoed the rattle and clatter of a coach-and-four. I looked up, still absently bouncing, then stopped.

It was by far the most elaborate contraption I had ever seen, its sides gilded and carved with coats of arms and arabesques. The coachman himself might have been royalty, so vivid was his livery, and the horses—I knew horses—were easily worth that man's yearly salary, each one of them. I did not yet know it, but my fortunes were about to take a turn from a chance meeting with the Marquis and Marquise Boullainvillers.

As the conveyance approached us, it slowed to a crawl. I could see now that in addition to the coachman, there was a footman stationed in back. Surely whomever it was that rode inside this marvelous contraption would have the breeding and intelligence to recognize me for who I was, the descendant of His Majesty Henri II? I determined at that moment to make their acquaintance, and by the subtlest of means garnered their attention.

The Marquise shrieked like a birthing mare when I leaped onto the side of the coach, pressing my dirty face against the glass. There was an ornamental gold lamp affixed above the window. I grabbed it, striving to balance myself and the baby with my free hand as I yanked as hard as I could at the lamp. With a snap it broke free. I jumped from the coach, splashing through frozen ruts until I reached the road's edge, where I veered off through the snow. Behind me I could hear the coachman shouting to his team to halt, and the cries of the footman as he jumped down and began to chase after me.

"Come back here, you little brigand!" he shouted.

With a curse he slipped and fell into the snow. I stopped and turned, covering my mouth to keep from laughing; and at that moment was grabbed by the shoulder.

It was the coachman.

" 'Tis only a girl," he called back to the waiting carriage. "And a baby. Come along, then—"

He took the lamp from me, shaking his head, and brought me to the coach. The door was open; he glanced inside, then back at me and said, "Don't you move, little thief."

He called out to the footman, directing him to repair the lantern; then looked down at me once more.

"In you go—"

I had been inside a coach before, of course, but never one so grand as this. And never while dressed in rags, my face splotched with soot and filth, and with a baby on my back. I hesitated, but the coachman's face, while stern, was not cruel — unlike that of the footman, who scowled at me as he wiped dirty snow from his breeches. I lifted my head defiantly, reached around to free my sister from her bundle so that she could toddle beside me, and clambered up the steps into the carriage.

There are round, well-fed faces that are inherently kind, and finely-dressed figures as generous as any alms-giver. It is a fact forgotten during the Reign of Terror, that poverty breeds misery, and misery when it looks upon misery reacts as a starving dog will, snarling and biting and even devouring helpless pups. Whereas warmth and wealth can breed charity even toward the most rawboned stray.

So it was with the Marquis and Marquise Boullainvillers. As I entered the carriage I saw the Marquise first. She was a handsome woman of many years, perhaps forty-four or forty-five, clad in a luxuriously thick cape of dark-patterned velvet, a Belgian lace collar frothing about her neck and Belgian lace cuffs above black velvet gloves. Her plump face still showed a warm beauty, and the heavy, fashionable jet-and-silver earrings glinting from the folds of her hood showed that her husband, or some other man, continued to hold her in his regard.

At this very moment, however, that regard was

fixed upon me: the Marquis Boullainvillers, as expensively clad as his wife but with a lean, rather pinched face, was gazing at me with an expression of detached distaste, as though I were a large, probably harmless insect that had bumbled into his view.

"You have searched her?" he called out to the coachman.

The coachman diligently appeared behind me and began to go through my pockets. My baby sister clutched my leg, staring at him with huge round eyes. Meanwhile the Marquise gazed at me curiously. Finally she spoke.

"Where are your parents, my dear?"

Her tone was so kind it shamed me. I looked away, and the Marquis nudged me with his ivory-handled walking stick.

"Speak up, child. Don't keep us waiting."

I kept them waiting. There is a demon in me sometimes, that is what my old nurse used to say. The coachman continued his search for stolen goods, and suddenly gave a grunt of triumph: he had discovered the rolled-up parchment hidden in the sleeve of my sweater. I grabbed at it but he was too big and too strong: he held me at arm's-length and handed the genealogy chart to the Marquise.

"That is mine!" I cried. "You have no right to touch it!"

The Marquise ignored me, gingerly unrolling the

chart and reading it. Her carefully plucked eyebrows rose as she glanced up at me in surprise.

"A Valois?"

Her husband removed a monocle from his breast pocket and proceeded to study the chart as well.

"It is a street sham," he announced a minute later. "A street sham used to gain sympathy."

My demon acted for me then. Before the Marquis could utter another word, I kicked him, hard, in the knee and grabbed my scroll. With a howl of pain he raised his walking stick to strike me. I bared my teeth, prepared to kick him again, and harder this time, when without warning the Marquise rose from her seat. Like a vast velvet cloud she hovered between me and her husband, glowering at him until he lowered the walking stick. Then, as though she and I were alone in the carriage, she turned back to me.

"Such a pale little thing," she said softly, gazing down at my little sister. "May I . . . ?"

She reached to touch *mon ange*, and I drew my arm protectively about her. The poor creature began to whimper. The Marquise clucked to herself, then tilted her head and gave me a look. It was a look that betokened trust, and standing there with this stranger, I knew somehow that she *was* to be trusted. I said nothing but nodded. The Marquise stroked the baby's cheek, then frowned.

"This poor cherub is roasting with fever!" she exclaimed. "This child needs caring for."

I whirled and knelt beside my sister, cradling her to me. The Marquise gently stroked the poor mite's head, her beringed fingers smoothing hair damp and matted with sweat. After a moment she glanced back at the Marquis, smiling.

"I daresay it might be invigorating to have children about for a time," she said.

Her husband's scowl indicated he did not share this sentiment. He straightened his waistcoat, cleared his throat, and had just begun to open his mouth when the Marquise glared at him.

"Don't you agree?" she said icily.

And that was all it took. Minutes later the baby was ensconced upon the Marquise's lap, cooing happily as she patted at the dowager's jet earrings. Beside her the Marquis sat, scowling as he rubbed his bruised knee. As for me—I sat in the satin-covered seat across from them, admiring the ivory broach on our benefactress's impressive bosom, and the rubies stitched onto the brocade cuffs of the Marquis's jacket. At his fierce frown I looked away, turning my attention to the satin cushions beneath me, the gilt tassels that hung by the window: all the sumptuous trappings of the Parisian elite, spread out for my delectation.

And so it was that I was taken under the patronage of the Marquis and Marquise Boullainvillers. To me, as well as to all who knew them, these two represented the very apex of style and grandeur. By their grace I shared in this, and through their unfailing kindness and patronage, over the next fifteen years I was to receive a glimpse into the most rarefied reaches of true, elevated society.

I daresay a glimpse was all that I needed . . .

Chapter

FOUR

❧ ✦ ❧

Of all the glories of the Palace of Versailles—the fabled gardens, the Hall of Mirrors, the Galeries des Glaces and the countless staterooms and galleries and chapels—the loveliest and most treasured by Her Majesty Queen Antoinette was the Petit Trianon. A neoclassical pavilion erected by her husband, Louis XVI, back when the King and Queen were still adolescent rulers of what they imagined might be a fairy-tale realm, the Petit Trianon was hidden in the expansive gardens of Versailles, a mile from the palace. Marie Antoinette herself oversaw its decoration, filling its sunlit rooms with roses and lilies of the valley and other delicate blossoms, all specially grown in the palace greenhouses. Silk tapestries embroidered with more flow-ers covered the walls, *petite-point* carpets bloomed like a garden underfoot, and Her Majesty's beloved pug dogs capered and slept on satin and velvet cushions scented with crushed violets and dried rose petals.

It was at the Petit Trianon that Marie was ever happiest. It was here that she entertained her dear-est friends at late night soirees, after the tedious business of the day had passed; and it was here on a cloudless evening in early spring that Her Majesty herself had taken the stage in the pavilion's tiny jewel-box theater. Outside, carriages and cabri-olets crowded the small courtyard. Footmen gam-bled or gossiped, awaiting the return of their masters and mistresses, and exchanging news of who was out of favor, who on the rise, and who al-ready had been cut dead by Her Majesty that after-noon at Mass.

Inside, however, one might mistake the fabulous gowns and glittering Venetian glass chandeliers for the setting of a fairy play. And indeed a play of sort was in progress. Upon the Petit Trianon's match-box-sized stage, Her Majesty was beguiling her guests with a song. Arms uplifted to display every shining inch of her glorious gown, its pleats and folds of aquamarine silk cascading about her in a haze of pale blue and gray and silver, seed-pearls and aquamarine gems dazzling in the candlelight. Her powdered wig extended a full foot above her heart-shaped face, and atop its confectionery curls

swayed a fan-shaped headdress of white and ultramarine ostrich plumes. Behind her, costumed actors
executed the steps of a galliard, moving carefully
between the stage curtains. Her Majesty was sup-
posed to be in a wood, her voice nightingale-sweet as
she sang of the glories of love.

"The Queen is in fine voice tonight." Near the
front of the stage, a dowager of the old realm—
Madame Pomfre—lowered her fan to murmur to
the much younger man beside her. "The role of a
temptress suits her."

The young man made a lewd gesture, smiling
slyly back at her. "No doubt it is a role our Antoinette has played before."

Madame Pomfre feigned embarrassment, quickly
turning her attention back to the stage as Her
Majesty extended her arms in a sweeping gesture.
As the last notes echoed through the little theater,
thousands of white rose petals fell in a fragrant
shower from overhead. The assembled audience of
elegantly dressed courtiers burst into delighted
gasps and then spirited applause. The young man,
Retaux de Vilette, joined in, cheering. He leaned
over to say something to his companion, then
halted, his attention captured by a figure moving
tentatively through a rose-petal curtain in the back
of the theater.

"Now, who might *that* interesting little tart belong to?" he whispered.

Madame Pomfre turned with difficulty, her wig

wobbling atop her head. The young woman in question was perhaps twenty-four, slender, and simply coiffed. Her dress was modest compared to the fabulous displays around her, but the glowing crimson silk and scalloped décolletage suited her black hair and pale skin. Her face had an austere, almost intimidating presence, exotic and beautiful rather than merely pretty—strongly chiseled jaw, high cheekbones, slanting leonine eyes and a wide slash of a mouth that was softened somewhat by a full, rather tremulous lower lip.

She hesitated and gazed uncertainly around the room. That alone marked her as a newcomer, thought Retaux. Everyone knew that at Versailles one *seized* without hesitation one's rank and position, lest it fall into another's hands, and one behaved the same way toward finding a place in the Petit Trianon's tiny theater. He watched as the young woman made a move toward an empty seat, only to be rebuffed as a cool-eyed Duchess played her fan upon the cushion, indicating that the pretty interloper was not welcome there. The dark-haired girl only lifted her chin defiantly and joined the lesser courtiers where they stood along the aisles.

"She goes by the name La Motte," sniffed Madame Pomfre. "Countess, no less. She claims to be a member of the royal House of Valois."

Retaux de Vilette smirked. "What is possibly to be gained by such a ridiculous assertion?"

Madame Pomfre glanced at him sideways, playfully brushing his cheek with her fan. "Perhaps, quite simply, it is the truth."

"The truth?" Retaux gazed back at her, his lips parted in amazement. "What a novel approach."

He turned his attention back to the young Comtesse de La Motte, who was staring transfixed at the figure of Marie Antoinette cavorting onstage with a handsome young actor. "Her dress teeters rather unsteadily upon the edge of this season's fashion," Retaux remarked dryly to his companion. "Her eyes, though—very exciting."

Madame Pomfre took his chin in her hand and turned his face toward her. "Be mindful of who you came with tonight," she said warningly.

Retaux's beautiful mouth curled into a seductive *moue*. "As if it were possible to forget," he purred.

Madame Pomfre smiled. She leaned toward him, opening her fan so that it hid their faces as she drew him closer, to take her pleasure of that handsome, practiced mouth.

⋙ LATER, AFTER THE THEATRICAL ENTERTAIN-ment was finished, the Queen's courtiers gathered outside the pavilion, to gossip and take refreshments. It was a clear evening: stars shone brightly in a sky the color of lilacs. The first young pale leaves of lindens and chestnut trees formed a delicate tracery behind the Petit Trianon's eaves. Costumed actors pranced and swayed among the crowd, amusing them with sleight of hand and snippets of poetry composed especially for the occasion. A woman disguised as a peacock stepped regally from the pavilion steps, her own beauty hidden behind a feather mask and the ultramarine plumes which hugged her nearly naked torso.

Near the steps, Retaux de Vilette stood, sipping champagne from a glass frosted with castor sugar and preserved violets. He smiled as the peacock passed. She dipped her head toward him, her eyes heavy-lidded, and indicated that he might follow her behind a topiary hedge.

"Perhaps later," Retaux murmured, and with a flutter of her false feathers the peacock stalked off.

Retaux went back to perusing the crowd. There was Monsieur Caloné, that *effete poseur* with his shrill laugh; there Madame Vermont, until recently out of favor due to a bit of gossip involving herself and a chambermaid—though her presence here tonight suggested that situation may have changed. There was Monsieur Breteuil, Her Majesty's formidable House Minister, his scowl as much a fixture as the gray powdered wig that clung to his forehead. There was Mademoiselle Giraud—Retaux licked a fleck of castor sugar from his lips and smiled, recalling an afternoon on the lake with Mademoiselle Giraud—and *there* was Monsieur Giraud, the young lady's father.

Retaux quickly looked away. As he did, his gaze

fell upon the figure he had been searching for, the slender dark-haired woman with the feline eyes and crimson dress. She was alone at the edge of the crowd, pacing back and forth and staring anxiously at the steps of the Trianon.

Retaux handed his glass to a passing servant and took a step toward the young countess. If he were to move, so, he would be in her line of sight; but before he could draw closer the crowd began to stir and shift excitedly.

Retaux turned. On the terrace above him, the Queen and her troupe of actors had stepped from the interior darkness. The throng below applauded, and to their delight the Queen made a deep bow.

"It was an evening of triumph, yes?" she called in her clear fluting voice, and a wave of cheering told her that yes, it had been a triumph. Smiling, the Queen stepped from the terrace. The members of her inner circle clustered around her as she began to make her way through the assembled courtiers, stopping now and then to receive a compliment, or bestow one.

Retaux watched her, marveling as always at not just how regal, but how *professional* Antoinette was—her every gesture, smile, or wink conveyed as much meaning as the most practiced posturing of an actor in the *Comedie Francaise*. She had just reached a small claque of twittering young women whose hairpieces towered precariously above them, when Retaux's reverie was abruptly broken.

From her post near the topiary hedge, the Comtesse de La Motte was striding quickly and purposefully toward the Queen. Even from where he stood, Retaux could see how the young woman's eyes were glittering with grim determination.

Retaux frowned. He wasn't certain who might be in danger—the Comtesse? Her Majesty?—but the Comtesse's expression made him uneasy. He pressed through the crowd, calling out to her.

"Countess—"

She did not hear. Around him the crowd surged toward the Queen. Retaux took a deep breath and shoved his way past a fat dowager, in time to see Jeanne reach into the satin reticule that hung from her waist.

"Countess," he repeated, but helplessly this time: he was too far away. He could only watch as the young woman launched herself toward the Queen, falling to her feet in a swoon as Antoinette passed. In the Comtesse's hand a parchment scroll was clutched like an extinguished torch.

Without so much as a glance at the fallen girl, Antoinette swept past, flicking her skirt as she went. Behind Her Majesty, House Minister Breteuil started toward the Comtesse, his face scarlet with rage.

Retaux was there before him. He propelled himself through the scattering crowd and knelt beside her. "You dear frail creature," he murmured, and patted her cheeks—a little more roughly, perhaps, than a genuinely frail creature deserved.

Jeanne de La Motte's eyes opened. She grabbed his hand and held it at arm's length from her face. "I have only had a faint, Monsieur," she snapped. "You need not revive me from the dead."

Retaux said nothing, only watched as she looked past him at the departing royal entourage. Antoinette laughed gaily, rapping the hand of a courtier with her fan, then turned and disappeared into the darkness.

"You again." Jeanne de La Motte sat up as Minister Breteuil loomed over her, scowling. "I've told you to maintain your distance from Her Majesty."

"Forgive me, House Minister." Jeanne lowered her eyes modestly. "I was overcome by the strain of an important matter. One I believe the Queen would find of interest."

"You and all the rest," said Breteuil disdainfully. "At Versailles, distressed gentlefolk are as common as ragwort."

From behind him came tittering laughter: a handful of courtiers had remained to observe Breteuil at his work. Jeanne glanced at them, flushing, then said, "I have sought a proper audience, Monsieur, but always I am turned away."

Breteuil stared at her with utter contempt. "Her Majesty does not care to know you."

Jeanne stared back at him coldly. "I will hear that from her own lips."

The crowd gasped at this brazen response. As Breteuil's face darkened to violet, Retaux de Vilette cleared his throat and straightened. "House Minister. This is not worthy of your attention. Allow me to handle the Countess."

Breteuil stared at him, his lips curled. Abruptly he nodded. "See to it that I do not," he said, and hurried after the royal entourage.

Retaux waited until the House Minister was gone, and then turned to gaze back down at Jeanne de La Motte. "I am Retaux de Vilette," he said, gracing her with his most charming smile as he bowed. "Is there any way I may further assist you?"

Jeanne stared back at him. She saw a young man of about her own years, with unpowdered clear skin (not a trace of the pox!), and dark brown hair with an auburn tinge. His own hair, she noted approvingly, thick and lightly powdered; not one of those ghastly wigs that were *de rigeur* among those members of Louis XVI 's cohort who had already gone bald from the pox, or worse. A strong cleft chin; dark gray eyes; that finely drawn mouth Madame Pomfre had made such good use of earlier.

A smile began to play about her own mouth. "Is there any way that you may assist me?" she said, taking Retaux's hand and letting him help her to her feet. "Why, we must see to it that there is."

Chapter

FIVE

~⚜~

They rode in his carriage through the city of Versailles. To prolong the pleasure of his time with the enchanting young countess, Retaux had discreetly directed the coachman to take the longest route to her residence. This brought them through some of the seedier and more disreputable parts of the city, but Retaux was not concerned. His skill with rapier and pistol had been honed during numerous encounters—formal and otherwise—with unhappy fathers and cuckolded husbands.

And there was always the chance that the alarming sights *outside* the carriage might send an easily frightened young thing into the arms of the man *inside* of it.

The Comtesse de La Motte, however, did not seem to be that sort of young woman. Indeed, as the carriage rolled past a bonfire where vagrants had gathered to watch an impromptu performance by a troupe of street actors, Jeanne leaned closer to the window.

"Oh, do ask him to slow down!" she exclaimed, lips parted in amusement as she gazed outside. "Look!"

Retaux obeyed, and the coach slowed. He drew beside Jeanne to see what had captivated her.

In the street a man played the violin. Behind him a makeshift stage had been set up, with garish sets and cheap cotton emblazoned with the royal coat of arms standing in for the marvels of Versailles. On stage pranced two women, singing and gesticulating as the crowd roared. Their breasts threatened to spill from their scarlet bodices, and when they pulled up their skirts to reveal crimson stockings and a flash of bare white thigh, the crowd erupted in cheers. A pair of actors wearing cartoonish parodies of court dress chased them across the stage, while two tiny poodles capered after them, yapping and dancing on their hind legs.

"Rather less refined than our entertainment earlier this evening," sniffed Retaux.

"Wait," said Jeanne.

As she spoke the flimsy back-curtain parted. A woman emerged, a good eight feet tall, her voluminous skirts trembling as she walked carefully to the edge of the stage. Retaux sucked his breath in sharply in amazement.

The woman's vulgar makeup and garish costume notwithstanding, she bore an uncanny, almost supernatural resemblance to the Queen.

"Antoinette and Madame Campan,
Together they did sup.
The Queen's hungry tongue did lick and lap
Deep inside her lady's loving cup . . ."

Retaux's astonished gasp turned to laughter as the chorus and Antoinette sang on.

"In the hay Her Majesty lay,
No matter if it 'twas rank.
Her legs were splayed, her all displayed
For Bonnervilles and Frank."

Jeanne stared at the vulgar impersonator, craning her neck as the carriage rumbled on.

And for one fleeting instant, the false Antoinette stared back. Their eyes met, and locked; then with a sudden jolt the carriage careened down an alley. Jeanne turned, her expression thoughtful, and saw Retaux gazing at her avidly.

"It never works, you know," he said. "Those little ploys to garner the Queen's attention."

Jeanne dipped her head, ignoring him. Retaux waited; when she did not reply he gestured at her reticule. The parchment scroll protruded from its opening.

"What is on the paper you were so eager to press into our sovereign's regal palm?"

Jeanne glanced down; then slowly removed the parchment and handed it to him. Retaux unfurled it carefully, smoothing it on his knees as the carriage bounced down the narrow alley. After a moment he looked up, letting the parchment roll back with a *snap*; and tossed the scroll back at Jeanne.

"Has this claim of your heritage been *authenticated*?" he asked teasingly.

Jeanne regarded him, saying nothing. At last she sighed. "It has not. The King's Minister of Titles refuses to see me. But I know the truth. My father's estate was usurped by intimates of the royal family. I wish to petition for our estate's return."

Retaux raised one perfect eyebrow. "By accosting Antoinette?"

Jeanne lifted her head haughtily. "Being a woman, the Queen will be more sympathetic to my situation. Once she learns of the injustice that my family has endured, she will exert influence with the King and—"

Retaux began to laugh, so hard that the carriage rang with it. Jeanne stared at him, baffled, until finally with a snort he managed to compose himself.

"Forgive me, Countess. But you are so fresh, so new, so—*deliciously* naive."

As Retaux fell into a new fit of laughter, Jeanne's

bafflement darkened into anger. "It's remarkable how quickly you've made yourself tiresome," she said in a cold tone.

Retaux struggled to bring his amusement under control, wiping a tear from his eye. He reached into his vest pocket, to withdraw a handkerchief, Jeanne thought; but instead took out an elegant enameled snuffbox. He toyed with it absently, turning it this way and that, so that she could discern the portrait of a strikingly beautiful woman painted on its lid.

"I must ask myself," Retaux said, replacing the snuffbox and fixing Jeanne with his melting gaze, "why such a clever and alluring woman is without an escort? The Count must be old, and unable to attend to Madame's needs."

Jeanne flushed and looked away. "Count de La Motte is not yet thirty. He has retired from a triumphant career in the Cavalry. And I assure you," she added bitingly, "he attends my needs with vigor."

Retaux pretended great interest. "Indeed? I spent time in the Cavalry myself. I do not recall the Count."

"Perhaps he was in a regiment you were unfamiliar with," Jeanne replied, unruffled. She leaned out the window and called up to the coachman. "Stop here, driver."

They had come to the Place de Dauphine, by day a bustling area of inns and shops. Now, however, the square was empty save for a feral cat scavenging in a refuse heap. Without a word to Retaux, Jeanne stepped down from the carriage and hurried across the square. Retaux hesitated. Then with a gesture at the driver, he jumped out and gave pursuit.

By the time he caught up with her she was running up the steps of the Hotel Belle Image. Once a grand establishment, the little hotel had not seen prosperous times for several decades. Its tattered awning flapped disconsolately in the night wind, and a smell of stale cabbage and rancid water hung about the entryway.

"I must confess, Madame. I knew a Nicolas de La Motte in the Cavalry. But at the time he was no count. Then again, it is not uncommon for people to buy such titles."

Jeanne thrust past him into the building. "What you suggest is insulting, Monsieur de Vilette. It's even less attractive coming from a common gigolo."

Retaux followed her, unperturbed. "Ah. In that respect I fancy myself quite uncommon."

Inside, the hotel was dank and ill-lit, a single candle guttering in its filthy glass chimney, the carpeting underfoot soiled and damp. Jeanne swept up the stairs, pausing to stare warningly at her pursuer. "You've come too far, Monsieur. The Count is bad-tempered. If I call out, he will come."

Retaux met her gaze challengingly. "And do what?"

"Most likely separate you from the beloved tools of your trade."

"How disagreeable," Retaux murmured. He watched as Jeanne started back up the stairs, then called, "He is back, then?"

She hesitated but did not turn around. Retaux took a step after her and continued calmly, "I saw him not a week ago in Rambouillet. Strange though—he seemed quite rapt in the company of an actress from the Comedie."

Jeanne closed her eyes, composing herself, then went on. "Good night, Monsieur. Do not follow me."

It was not until she reached the door of her room that she looked over her shoulder. Before she could cry out, Retaux lunged from the shadows and grabbed her arm. Just as quickly Jeanne's hand whipped into her reticule to pull out a small pistol and thrust it against his cheek.

Retaux blinked; Jeanne cocked the glittering little gun, forcing him back against the rail on the landing. The rotted wood creaked dangerously, bending beneath his weight as Retaux craned his neck to stare two floors down.

"You inserted yourself into this situation, Monsieur," Jeanne hissed. "How do you propose to take leave of it?"

"Ahh." Retaux cleared his throat delicately, then whispered, "Have you any suggestions?"

"Find use for yourself on my behalf." The pistol's mouth bored into his cheek. "Quickly."

Behind him the railing quivered. Its creak became a groan, as the posts began to give way.

"Madame!" Retaux blurted desperately. "At court the trick to obtaining your desires is to first know what everyone else desires!"

"Yes?" Jeanne regarded him coolly. "And you have such knowledge?"

Retaux smiled nervously. "It is my second greatest talent."

Jeanne's face softened slightly. Retaux's smile grew broader and more confident; he lifted a hand to move the gun away.

"Non." The gun jabbed even harder against his cheek. "Make no mistake, Monsieur. I hold the power between us."

A moment passed as she held his gaze. Then Retaux nodded, and she lowered the gun. Without a backward glance she left him and entered her rooms. Drawing a deep breath, Retaux looked down at the still-quivering stair rail, then turned and took a step toward Jeanne's chamber.

She stood just inside the door, lighting a single candle. When it flared into life he could see her living area, small and sparsely furnished with a few chairs, a spindly table, and a half-opened trunk from which spilled the folds of a rose-patterned dressing gown. Against the far wall a Chinese screen hid a rumpled bed. Retaux glanced at it, then at Jeanne de La Motte. She lifted her head to smile at him, then gently but firmly closed the door in his face.

Chapter

SIX

❧❦

Y our Majesty. This is the culmination of my life's work."

Outside the Queen's sitting room, sunlight glistened on the swelling buds of lilacs and dwarf apple trees, and sent silvery ripples across the surface of an ornamental pond where a single swan floated, nibbling at duckweed. A brief morning shower had left the new young leaves of lindens and crab apples brilliant as though dipped in ice. A few droplets still coursed down the leaded glass windows, so that all seemed suspended within a gigantic prism.

Inside, Her Majesty's chamber was no less glittering beneath a Venetian glass chandelier lit, despite the early hour, with a hundred beeswax candles. Antoinette sat upon the window seat, embroidering a Belgian lace handkerchief with her initials, the letters tiny and precise as a spiderweb. Nearby her lady-in-waiting, Madame Campan, perched on a cushion doing needlepoint.

And in the center of the room stood Monsieurs Bohmer and Bassenge, court jewelers to Her Majesty the Queen. It was Monsieur Bohmer who had first addressed her. Chief partner, he was a saturnine man of medium height, plump though exquisitely dressed in the royal livery, with fawn-colored lace peeking from the brocade cuffs of his jacket. The man beside him, thinner and with a pockmarked face, turned this way and that as Bohmer directed, so that Her Majesty could see the extraordinary creation of which Bohmer spoke.

It was a necklace. Though to call it that suggested that it might be compared to other necklaces, other confections brought by Her Majesty's jewelers. And the truth was that Antoinette—with all her cases of bijoux, her bracelets and tiaras and rings and armlets, her emerald collars and sapphire-studded wristlets—Antoinette had never seen anything like this.

"It consists of 647 brilliants of the first water," Monsieur Bohmer announced, his finger tracing an arabesque in the air before him. "The weight of it in its entirety is no less than 2800 carats."

As he spoke, Bassenge slowly caressed the streams of diamonds on his waistcoat. It was the type of necklace then in vogue and called a *rivière*, because of the glittering flow of its jewels. A gaudy form of jewelry, favored by actresses who in turn had been favored by wealthy men, the *rivière* might be considered a trifle extreme for a ruler whose people had recently known famine.

But Antoinette was notorious for her extreme tastes. She already owned other jewels created by Bohmer and Bassenge—a spray of diamonds and aquamarines, a diamond bracelet, a pair of chandelier earrings.

These might have been made of paste, when held beside the necklace before her. It fell in tier upon tier of shimmering blue and white and spectral green brilliants, mimicking the glow of the chandelier overhead. Antoinette looked up from her embroidery, her lips parted, and shook her head.

"Well, Monsieur Bohmer. It is a marvel."

Bohmer laughed, giddy with pleasure, and clapped his hands together. "Thank you. I assure you, Monsieur Bassenge and I have put our very souls into the piece."

"And every *livre* you possess, I'll wager," said the Queen.

Bohmer laughed again, uneasily this time. "Naturally, we occurred some, er, *debt* in the purchase of the stones."

Behind them the door opened. Colleen, one of the Queen's pretty young chambermaids, peered inside.

"Shall I clean now, Your Majesty?"

The Queen gave her a sharp look, and Colleen quickly left. Antoinette turned calmly back to her piecework.

"I'm certain you'll have no trouble finding a buyer, Monsieur Bohmer."

Bohmer's shrill laughter died away. "Our single greatest hope has always been that it would find its place with you."

Antoinette gave a quick glance at Madame Campan, who raised her eyebrows slightly. "How curious," said the Queen. "It was suggested to me that this piece was originally destined for Madame Du Barry."

Bohmer drew a hand to his cheek in a show of ignorance. "Madame Du Barry?"

The Queen's pale eyes flashed angrily. "That trollop my husband's father maintained. You recall the woman, don't you, Madame Campan?" she demanded, turning to her lady-in-waiting.

"Vividly, Your Majesty." Madame Campan lifted clear gray eyes from her needlework. "A creature of extravagant tastes and an eye for the ostentatious." She turned to gaze at the jeweler, letting the unspoken accusation find its mark.

Monsieur Bohmer reddened. "Well, I—that is, we, we—"

"I pray that the rumors of this necklace's provenance are mere court gossip," Antoinette went on with studied casualness. "Otherwise, Du Barry's recent banishment from court would find you without a buyer."

"If Your Highness would permit," Monsieur Bassenge broke in, "we are foggy on the exact order of events that led to its creation. But this in no way diminished our desire that the necklace should become Your Majesty's own."

Bohmer nodded eagerly and bounced toward him. "I concur!" he cried, removing the *rivière* from Bassenge's neck. "If Her Majesty would try the necklace on, perhaps—"

He swiveled, holding out the jewels and stepping clumsily toward the Queen. He froze as Antoinette raised her hand, commanding him to stop. For an instant she gazed at the glittering waterfall suspended before her, and the diamonds sent flickers of white and blue and crimson sparking across her face.

"It *is* a phenomenon," she admitted at last. "And you are to be commended. Still, I decline. France needs ships right now, Monsieur Bohmer. Not necklaces."

"We are the appointed jewelers to Her Majesty!" Bohmer's voice rose to a squeak. "Our reputations will be shattered if we are forced to seek other buyers!"

The Queen turned away. "I did not commission this necklace. I do not wish to acquire it. I need not explain myself further."

Bohmer's mouth opened, but Bassenge touched

him on the arm, shaking his head almost imperceptibly. Bohmer nodded, once, then stiffly crossed the room to replace the necklace in its velvet case. The two men stood by the door, then bowed. For another moment it looked as though Bohmer would speak again, but Antoinette's icy stare silenced him. Without another word the two jewelers left.

In the sudden quiet Antoinette carefully threaded her needle through the corner of a silken handkerchief, then raised her head to catch Madame Campan's droll expression. As though they were two schoolgirls ridiculing a clumsy master, they burst into peals of laughter.

❧ THERE WAS NO LAUGHTER WITHIN JEANNE'S head or heart as she waited, Retaux at her side, within the airless confines of the receiving room to the Office of the Minister of Titles. Around them numerous courtiers sat—every one of them a man, Jeanne noted with distaste and not a little anxiety. She glanced up, and saw overhead a bluebottle banging itself desultorily at the ceiling. She watched for several minutes until at last it fell, exhausted, to the floor near her feet. Jeanne gazed at the fly sympathetically, and winced when one of the Minister's scribes scurrying ceaselessly back and forth crushed it beneath his feet. She sighed, closing her eyes and trying to imagine that she was in some other, cooler, place—alone.

"Are you certain you want to do this?" Retaux's voice was low and filled with concern. Jeanne nodded without looking up.

"Yes."

One of the double doors leading to the Minister's office opened and a secretary swept into the waiting room, his powdered nose pointing skyward. Jeanne clasped her hands in her lap and stared at him hopefully; but he gazed past her, to one of the aristocrats sitting with the bored placid expression of a pug dog, and waved him in.

"He's not going to see me," Jeanne said slowly as the door closed once again. "I've tried, day after day I've tried . . ."

She struggled to keep despair from her voice, but could not help adding in a child's sad tones, "Why should today be any different?"

Retaux smiled. "Well—among other reasons, because the Minister of Titles' Aunt is an—*acquaintance* of mine."

Jeanne gave him a wan look. "Your resourcefulness is impressive."

Retaux toyed with his lace cuff. "Like so many of my other gifts, I learned it from the self-proclaimed Duchess d'Vossi."

"Someone else's cherished aunt?" asked Jeanne teasingly.

"No. My mother," Retaux replied in a matter-of-fact tone, "who was a whore. And a very good one," he added, raising an eyebrow at Jeanne's stunned look. "Does that shock you?"

"Well, no—I mean, I—"

Retaux went on gracefully, trying to put her at ease. "Under the Duchess's tutelage, one quickly learned to fend for one's self. And to bow—" He nodded almost imperceptibly at one of the courtiers dozing across the room. "—to the well-mannered gentlemen who came to call. At least she left me something," he ended sadly.

Jeanne stared at him for a long moment. "I'm sorry," she said at last.

Retaux shook his head, as though dispersing the memory of a dream, then smiled at her.

"We all earn our place here, Countess," he said. "One way or another."

At his intense gaze Jeanne turned away, hoping he would not see her cheeks color; grateful he could not read her wistful thought: *How alike we are, Retaux and I . . .*

He said nothing more. The hours passed, heat and silence, the occasional cough or snort from a sleeping courtier, the relentless pad of feet as the scribes ran back and forth, back and forth. The Minister's office door opened and shut, the secretary's head popped in and out like Harlequin in a puppet show; names were called, a veritable litany of aristocrats old and newly minted; but the name was never Jeanne de La Motte. At last, as the light in the high windows deepened from amber to gold, the room was empty save for Jeanne and Retaux, and the dead bluebottle on the floor. Jeanne stared at the tiny crushed corpse, disheartened, her eyes starting to ache; when she glanced at Retaux beside her, he too seemed to have lost faith in his gambit.

When the office door once more creaked open, she did not even look up; it was not until Retaux grasped her hand and whispered urgently, "Jeanne! He's calling for you!" that she realized it was indeed her name being pronounced by the secretary, with as much weariness and disdain as though her were summoning the dead fly.

"Comtesse?" He stared at her, then motioned reluctantly at the door.

Jeanne stood, gathering her skirts and giving Retaux a quick smile as she hurried into the office.

Like the waiting room, the Minister's office had seen better times. The last traces of gilt had flaked from the wainscoting, leaving smudges like handprints. The ornately carved outer wall wore a verdigris film of mildew and cobwebs. Where the shelves had not buckled from their weight, books and scrolls were crammed from ceiling to floor; where the wood had finally given way, all of these had fallen and lay strewn about the dusty floor—birth records, death records, family histories, titles, claims, deeds, wills, crests. Within all this the Minister of Records himself sat behind an enormous desk even more cluttered with the refuse of time and the mortal desire to conquer it, parchments and elaborate renderings of family trees.

He was bent so that Jeanne could only glimpse his face beneath its wig and the long, somewhat moldering plume of the quill pen that scribbled furiously across the pages of an immense ledger. She waited, silent, for him to acknowledge her; so intent was he upon his work that she gradually became certain he did not, in fact, know that she was in the room with him. Her lips had barely parted for her to timidly address him when he spoke first.

"I am aware of your presence." He did not bother to look up. "I can hear you thinking."

Jeanne flushed. Had she known that Retaux was watching her, from where the secretary had left the office door ajar, even the Minister of Titles might have taken notice.

"Th–thank you for seeing me," she said haltingly. "You don't know how long I have waited for this opportunity."

Now at last the Minister set aside his quill. He gazed at Jeanne with mild disdain, his austere features rendered even more intimidating by his evident lack of anything but the faintest interest in her or her plight.

Jeanne took in his cold contempt; then quickly, before she could lose her nerve, stepped toward him.

"Please, Minister. Tell me—have you considered my petition?"

The Minister sat, silent; picked up a petition from the heap upon his desk and regarded it with distaste. He stepped out from behind his desk, studying the parchment as he paced slowly across the room.

"It is unusual for you to come here on your behalf," he said with what might have been a grudging flicker of interest. "In my experience, women do not possess the temperament for negotiations."

Jeanne felt her cheeks burn even more; before she could blurt out a protest she lowered her eyes, pretending modesty as she stared at the floor. The Minister took no notice; only stopped before the dust-glazed window. Here several glass bell jars stood in a neat row; beneath each belled top was a Venus flytrap, its leaves opening like tiny green-and-crimson hands improbably and disconcertingly lined with serrated teeth.

"It would be more appropriate for me to discuss this with Count de La Motte," he said, and reached for an atomizer on the sill. "Why has he not come?"

"My husband is in Rambouillet," Jeanne replied—quickly, she realized as the Minister cast her a sharp glance. "In any event, it is my lineage I wish to have authenticated, not his. It is my family's home I wish returned— to me."

The Minister of Titles said nothing. He bent over a small table by the window, picking up a small jar and a pair of tweezers. As Jeanne watched in growing disgust, he used the tweezers to pluck several squirming beetles from the jar and proceed to drop them, one by one, into the Venus flytraps.

"Your petition places me in a difficult position," he said after several minutes had passed. "Your father was prone to stirring up Parliament—"

"He spoke against poverty and tyranny," said Jeanne calmly.

"Your father was a treacherous liar!" Jeanne recoiled as the Minister turned on her, his face scarlet. "Nothing more!"

"He was a man who only wanted to better the world around him!" Jeanne said, barely keeping her voice from shaking. "If there were more men—or women!—like him at Versailles—"

Her arm swept out despairingly, striking a pile of neatly arranged documents on the Minister's desk. The Minister looked startled; with fierce chagrin Jeanne attempted to restrain herself.

"Forgive me," she said, and hastened to straighten the fallen documents.

The Minister watched her; then, as though not wanting to be outdone, he inclined his head to her and said in a more even tone, "He railed against the monarchy—and that will *never* be tolerated."

"Monsieur." Jeanne replaced the last bit of parchment and turned to him imploringly. "You of all people know the importance of a God-given name, and a home in which it can flourish. It *defines* us."

The Minister shook his head. "Your request is no doubt from the heart, Comtesse; but there are higher considerations . . ."

"I implore you, Minister! If I have no legacy to pass on, the name of Valois dies with me!"

The Minister continued to stare at her, as though waiting for her to reply to a question he had secretly uttered. At last he said, "In the eyes of the Royal Family, that would not be an unfavorable result. This royal office—" He turned and walked back to his desk. "—will not grant your pardon. It never will."

Jeanne gazed at him crestfallen, wondering if somehow she had misheard his sentence. It was not until he said, "Good day, Comtesse," and gestured at the door that she realized that her interview, at last, was over.

❧ SHE FOUND RETAUX WAITING FOR HER IN the anteroom. He gave no sign of having overheard her conversation with the Minister, only rested a gentle hand upon her shoulder as she stood despairingly by the window.

"There is no reason for me to stay," she said, shaking her head sadly. "I will not accomplish what I came to do."

Retaux let his hand move from her shoulder down to the smooth arc of her jaw. His fingers cupped her chin as he lifted her face to his and stared, smiling, into her sorrowful face.

"There are other ways," he said, his smile broadening into a devilish grin. "Just you come with me, dear Comtesse—

"I will begin to teach them to you."

Chapter

S E V E N

~❧~

The next day, the surface of the lake near the Palace of Versailles shone clear and blue as blown glass beneath a periwinkle sky. A dozen or so swan boats plied their way across the smooth water, or rested alongshore beneath the pale yellow leaves of weeping willows. Now and then a courtier would call laughing from one boat to another, or offer a jesting challenge to a lady lying half-asleep in the bow while her companion paddled gently through the soft afternoon haze. An observer standing on shore would not mark any difference between the swan boat steered by Retaux de Vilette and any other—a handsome young man manning the paddle, a lovely young woman reclining as she watched.

Yet what passed between Retaux and Jeanne de La Motte was not mere courtship: it was education.

"The Marquis de Favras, third cousin of the Duc d'Orleans." Retaux raised his paddle to indicate a swan boat containing a foppish man in velvet breeches and powdered hair. "He likes games of chance, detests the opera, and has an appetite for young men."

Jeanne lifted her head to observe the Marquis, nodded at Retaux and sank back.

"The Comte d'Blonde," said Retaux as another boat approached. "Keeper of the Royal Seals. He is inept at his position and enthusiastically pursues any and all members of the female gender."

Once again Jeanne rose, to stare at a gentleman so fat that his boat listed alarmingly to one side as he leered at a passing young woman. When he lifted his wineglass to her, he nearly swamped his own craft. Retaux shook his head. "I cannot imagine why he bothers. He's as virile as an empty sausage skin."

"What about him?" asked Jeanne, noting a handsome youth who sat and admired two giggling countesses attempting to row him to the far shore.

"Pierre Charron, hero of the Battle of Haussman. He has killed four men in duels, loves stag hunting, and despite his overt flirtations maintains but a single lover—"

Jeanne leaned forward expectantly, as Retaux pointed his paddle in the opposite direction. "—the Marquis de Favras," he said, grinning at Jeanne's expression of disgust.

"Lechers and parasites," she said. "Is that all there is to be had?"

"Welcome to court." Retaux made a mock half-bow, and dipped the paddle into the blue water. "Here, appearance is everything. And I mean no offense, Countess, but yours is lacking. Your manner of dress—and your living arrangements—must improve."

Jeanne looked down, so that he would not see her flush, and tugged self-consciously at the frayed lace of her dress. Retaux shook his head and continued. "Plainly said, you need money. And to obtain it, you will need to find favor with someone who has it. Otherwise you will make little headway here."

As he spoke, a swan boat bearing three elderly dowagers drifted past. One of them called out to Retaux in a quavering voice, "Retaux, my precious!"

Retaux stood and greeted them with a bow. "Look ho! Three alluring sirens of the sea!"

He blew a kiss to them, and the trio cackled in delight. Jeanne let her hand trail through the water, staring fixedly at the line of bubbles rippling behind it. "How long do you intend to suffer the whims of old women?" she asked at last.

Retaux shrugged. "Suffer? I bring joy into the hearts of venerable ladies. Why, I'm often moved to tears by their appreciation."

Jeanne looked up at him and burst into laughter. "You evade the question, Monsieur!" she cried, splashing him.

Retaux ducked, the boat rocking as he tried to shield himself. "I will answer!"

He set the paddle down and slid onto the seat beside Jeanne. She stared at him, then reached over and tenderly wiped a drop of water from his cheek. He gazed back at her, his face suddenly serious.

"I shall stop suffering the whims of older women when someone more intriguing enters my world," he said softly.

"Am I to suppose you have no one of consequence now?" Before he could move, her nimble fingers dipped into his vest pocket and withdrew the elegant little snuffbox. Holding it up to admire, Jeanne examined the beautiful woman's face painted on the lid. "To hold a woman's image so tight to your breast would suggest an intimate history."

Retaux gazed at the snuffbox fondly, and nodded. "Yes. There could be no relationship more intimate —"

He paused, looking slyly at Jeanne before finishing. "—than that with one's own mother."

Jeanne smiled, trying to keep relief from flooding her face, and handed him the box. He stared down at it, and momentarily his face clouded.

Jeanne reached to touch his hand. "You need not speak of it if it troubles you."

Retaux shook his head, too quickly; kissed the snuffbox and returned it to his pocket. "Not at all. I owe her everything."

He linked his hands behind his head and leaned

back in the boat, the sun touching his fine, smooth features with gold. "Who can say?" he murmured, glancing at a passing swan boat, its revelers shrieking drunkenly as they splashed at each other. "Any one of these drooling fops bobbing past us now might well be my father. An amusing thought. Don't you agree, Jeanne?"

Jeanne looked at him, surprised and touched by this gallant effort to conceal his hurt. She moved closer to him, and gently laid her head upon his shoulder. "How skillfully you play the rogue. Yet even you cannot mask such profound loneliness."

Retaux said nothing, only stroked her hair as he gazed thoughtfully into the bright sky. After a moment he turned to her.

"Are we that much alike, Countess?" he asked, his hand still lingering upon her brow. "Are we?"

Few of the other party-goers noted as their swan boat drifted away from the rest, to bob slowly up and down in the afternoon light.

Chapter

EIGHT

❧

Cardinal Louis de Rohan—Prince de Rohan, Grand Almoner of France, and member of one of the country's oldest and most noble families—was a man accustomed to having his way. At the moment this consisted of taking one of his prize Arabian stallions through its paces, within the vast and echoing equestrian stable of the House of Rohan. To a stranger, the stables themselves might have seemed a palace fit for the Cardinal, the most powerful religious figure in all of France. Immense painted canvases hung upon the walls; there were fresh flowers in vases of precious Chinese porcelain by the stable entrance, and lavender water sprinkled onto the sawdust twice daily, to mitigate the smells of dung and equine sweat. One of Rohan's palace musicians sat beside the ring, playing a cello as the Cardinal's mount kept time with the melancholy music.

And yet another attempt to beautify the stable stood within the center of the equestrian ring— Madame de Niess, a very young beauty whose youth did not preclude her from having already been corrupted by the Cardinal. She wore only a linen chemise, loosely knotted at the waist so that her breasts bounced free beneath the cloth as she playfully gave chase to the Cardinal. Whenever she tired she would stop, breathing heavily, and take a few sustaining sips of champagne before once more setting off in pursuit.

"Anyone can see how it consumes you!" she cried, giggling as Rohan maneuvered his stallion into a regal, high-stepping canter. "Do images of her spin in your head even now?" She set down her glass and whirled, her long dark curls streaming about her head. "In your fantasies does the Queen Bee sit in her golden hive, smoldering with thoughts of you?"

Rohan's eyes narrowed. He was a striking man of fifty-five, with an angular face, high forehead, and thick black hair that fit well with the air of arrogant, even sinister hauteur that he affected. Silently he pointed his riding crop at the young girl. Still giggling, she drained her champagne flute, then lay down in the center of the arena, folding her hands upon her breast and holding the glass there as though it were the stem of a funeral lily.

"There," Rohan whispered. He brought his riding crop down upon his mount's side, banged his heels into the steed's flanks, and charged at the girl. She did not flinch as the stallion leaped over her, clearing her breast by inches. With a low cry Rohan brought the horse around and charged again. This time the Arabian's hoof shattered the champagne glass, crystal fragments like snow filling the air.

With a triumphant laugh Madame de Niess stood, shaking shards of crystal from her hair and chemise. Rohan reined his horse in, patting its neck and gazing abstractedly at his latest mistress. With a mocking laugh she let her hair fall free about her shoulders and faced him.

"Why brood? Queen Bee Antoinette will never reciprocate your feelings. The dream will always fade like a mist, and you will forever be left to play your lifelong role—"

She met his troubled stare and smiled provocatively. "That of the unrequited fool!"

Rohan swung a leg over his saddle and in one graceful move dismounted. Madame de Niess's smile faded as he stalked toward her. Too late she turned to flee: he grabbed her hair and spun her around to face him. With the same practiced brutality with which he treated his mount, he took her chemise in his hands and tore it from her shoulders.

Madame de Niess struggled fruitlessly. The Cardinal dipped his head to her shoulder, and as she cried out bit her neck. With one gloved hand he found the ribbon at the front of her chemise and pulled it free, so that the white fabric fell away and her breasts were exposed. He stroked her nipple until it reddened, then twisted it roughly. Madame de Niess moaned, her own hands stroking the front of Rohan's riding breeches as he pressed himself against her.

"Ahem."

The sound of someone clearing his throat echoed through the arena like a tocsin. Rohan looked up sharply. His secretary, Abel Duphot, stood at the edge of the ring.

Rohan sighed. "Already?"

Duphot nodded and made a conciliatory gesture. "You know how they are when you're late."

Without a backward glance at the woman he had nearly ravaged, Rohan spun and walked away, leaving Madame de Niess to gather what remained of her clothes and find her own way back to the palace.

✎ CARDINAL ROHAN WAS NO LESS IMPOSING A figure serving Mass in the Chapelle de Versailles, though his vestments were more splendid than his equestrian gear. His violet and scarlet robes rustled softly, in counterpoint to the susurrus of countless burning candles and the muted replies of his congregation. High above the chapel's vaulted ceilings glittered with gold and silver mosaics aflutter with cherubim, seraphim, and assorted *putti*; in the pews behind the marble altar rail, a few members of the Royal Family's staff waited for their master and mistress to appear.

"In nomine Patris, et Spiritus Sancti..."

"Amen."

"Introibo ad altare Dei. Ad Deum qui laetificat."

In an otherwise empty vestibule, Retaux de Vilette and Jeanne de La Motte stood in the shadows, watching as the Cardinal raised and lowered the golden chalice, its glory mirroring that of the jeweled gold miter upon his head.

"Judica me, Deus, causum meam de gente non sancta..."

"Don't be misled by his pious inflection," Retaux whispered. "That is Louis de Rohan, Cardinal of all France and blood Prince of the infamous House of Rohan. You will never find a more influential clan. Or a more decadent one."

"...ad hoine iniquo, et doloso erue me. Quia tu es, Deus fortitudo mea..."

Jeanne moved closer, angling to get a better view of the wicked Cardinal, and felt Retaux's breath warm upon her cheek as he went on. "Rohan is a debaucher of epic proportions, even by the standards of our dear court. He gambles to excess, and his parties are extraordinary—they could put the

Queen herself to shame. He indulges in, shall we say, *orgiastic* affairs."

"... *quare me repulsüsti, et quare tristis incedo, dum affligit me inimicus* ..."

"Who would have ever thought piety could be so liberating?" murmured Jeanne.

From the back of the chapel a choir of young boys, some no more than four years old, raised their voices in a hymn so pure it made Jeanne's neck bristle. She and Retaux turned, just as the chapel doors swung open and the Royal Family arrived. Antoinette entered first, wearing a gown of silver and pale blue tissue, its front embroidered with tiny diamants and seed pearls. She was crowned with a relatively demure creation, a headdress of pale blue ostrich plumes, entwined with silver thread and with a single blue topaz gleaming above her brow, the size of a baby's fist. At her side walked the ten-year-old Princess Royal, Marie-Therese Charlotte, a miniature version of her mother with hands pressed tightly together in an attitude of prayer, followed by the six-year-old Dauphin, too frail to bear his parents' hopes for the future of the monarchy.

And next to Antoinette was the King himself, Louis XVI. A beefy, thick-bodied man, his face ruddy from pursuit of his favorite pastimes: hunting and assisting the royal builders and masons with their work. Perilously nearsighted (spectacles were not favored at court), the King disliked sifting through the piles of letters, pronouncements, and decrees that found their way to his desk each day; but he adored hard physical labor. Even now, navigating his way down the chapel aisle, he could not stop the constant process of inspecting his surroundings for signs of wall fracture, loose mortar, crumbling plaster, or incipient dry rot. Halfway into the church, he stopped, staring up at the chapel ceiling. As he did so, the heads of his family and their small army of stewards, advisors, ladies-in-waiting and nursemaids, all tilted as well.

"There is crumbling in that masonry!" Louis announced triumphantly. "I suspected as much—it wasn't mortared properly. It should be attended to in quick order, and—"

Antoinette stretched out one delicate, gloved hand toward him. "Mass first, my love?"

With a last longing look at the ceiling Louis placed his hand atop hers. The royal entourage inched forward.

"One never really *owns* a palace," Louis went on in a loud voice. "One simply maintains it until the next poor bastard takes possession."

"*Language*, Monsieur!" Antoinette scolded him. "This is a house of God!"

"Crumbling though it may be," Louis muttered. He took his place at the communion rail beside his wife.

"*Dominus vobiscum.*" Cardinal Rohan raised the

communion wafer to the immense jewel-encrusted crucifix on the altar, then bowed his head. *"Et cum spiritu tuo. Amen."*

The Cardinal turned and approached the King.

"Corpus Domino nostri Jesu Christi custodiat animam tuam iun vitam aetenam," he intoned, and placed the wafer upon the King's tongue. He moved next to Antoinette, took another wafer from its gold vesicle. *"Corpus Domino nostri Jesu Christi,"* he repeated.

"Now. Observe this," whispered Retaux de Vilette to Jeanne in the safety of the vestibule.

Antoinette did not lift her face toward the Cardinal to receive communion. Rohan stood there, the holy wafer held tight between his fingers, his expression taut.

". . . custodiat animam tuam iun vitam aetenam," he finished in a strong clear voice.

Still she refused to look at him, or at the Host he offered to her. For a moment all eyes were fixed on this unmoving tableau: the angry Cardinal, the stubborn, haughty Queen. Finally Rohan turned and gestured curtly for an attending priest to take his place at the rail.

Jeanne touched a finger thoughtfully to her lips. "There appears to be a chill between the Cardinal and the Queen," she whispered.

Retaux nodded. "Some years ago Rohan held the position of ambassador to Antoinette's native Austria. While there he bedded half the Austrian court—the female half. To some of his, er, *intimates* he jested that Antoinette's mother, the Empress, had begged to have her turn."

Jeanne pressed closer to the entry to the vestibule, trying to get a better view. As she did so, she caught Rohan trying yet again to make eye contact with the Queen.

It was no good. Held high, the ostrich plumes dancing mockingly close to his face, Antoinette turned away from him and walked back to her pew.

"She has cut him again!" Jeanne marveled.

Retaux stepped forward, placing his hand lightly on her waist. "Rohan boasted that he declined the Empress. He claimed that her fragile fortress walls could never withstand the roar of his mighty cannon. Word of the slander got back to Antoinette. She has never forgiven him, despite his desperate attempts to heal the rift."

Jeanne continued to study the Royal Family, her lips pursed. "If the Rohans are as powerful as you say, what need has he of her approval?"

"He wishes to follow in the footsteps of Richelieu, and become Prime Minister. Only the reigning monarchs can grant that desire."

"And Antoinette blocks his progress."

"At every turn."

Jeanne nodded slowly. Her gaze sharpened as she stared at the Cardinal, and imagined to what use a man like that might be put—an overwhelmingly ambitious, almost unimaginably powerful man, yet cursed with a great vulnerability.

"There is much to think about here," she said in a low voice, and stepped back into the shadows.

❧ SHE RETURNED TO HER APARTMENT. THERE was an entire armoire full of gowns there, hats and gloves and all the armaments of charm and deportment and seduction. She had never thought of it before as *arming* herself, of posturing; of hiding herself within a costume as within shadow.

Yet that was what she found herself doing as she stood before the mirror. Trying on one hat and then another, discarding this confection of feather and diamant for that: all the while seeing somewhere behind the reflection not a beautiful woman in damask and lace, but a young knight on errantry, bent on preserving honor and family and all she had ever lived for, and loved.

"My curiosity about Your Eminence overcame my sense of formality," she pronounced shyly, curtseying before her image; then frowned and began again. "My curiosity—my curiosity—"

She stared into the mirror, made a *moue* that looked only petulant. "My curiosity . . ."

She lowered her eyes, raised them; practiced a smoldering glance and, finally, the vixen's sharp smile and glitter, all white teeth and narrowed eyes. "My curiosity about Your Eminence . . ."

Something broke inside her then, seeing the creature in the mirror, not herself at all but a terrible stranger, beautiful and dangerous and cold.

She turned quickly away, stepped to the trunk beside her armoire, and for a moment stood there, staring at what lay on top of it—a faded quilted blanket, its surface frayed and worn by years, but carefully preserved; as though it were the knight's standard, carried into battle and borne home again, more precious for its journeying. She bent and picked it up, stroking her face with the soft worn fabric, and seeming to feel then another face beneath hers, a child's round cheeks and trusting gaze, the feel of a tiny hand plucking at her, not imploringly but reassuringly, giving her strength for what she must do.

"My curiosity about Your Eminence," she began again, and this time her voice was confident, an echo of strength beneath words. "My curiosity about Your Eminence has overcome my sense of formality . . ."

She placed the blanket back atop the trunk and went to choose her costume.

The office of Cardinal and Royal Almoner held responsibilities besides attending to the spiritual needs of the monarchy and seducing beautiful young women. And so it was that a few days later, Rohan found himself hosting fifty or so members of the aristocracy to a hunt on the expansive grounds of the House of Rohan. Tents and pavilions had been set up at the verge of the woods; in the near distance, the fortress-like walls of the Rohan family's ancient château rose like a brooding dream from the afternoon haze. A handful of ladies had joined the hunting party, picking their way carefully through the long grass and whispering to each other as they watched the Cardinal shoot. Most of the guests, however, had chosen to remain within the pavilions, there to gossip and sample glories from the Cardinal's exceptional chef and even more exceptional cellars.

"Ah!"

A tenderhearted lady cried out in commiseration as a brightly-colored pheasant rose into the air, only to be blasted from the sky by Rohan's gun. A plume of blue smoke arced where a moment before the pheasant had fluttered, and was dispersed by the breeze. One of Rohan's servants ran to collect the dead bird; another servant handed the Cardinal a loaded gun, took his discharged weapon and handed it to yet another servant, to be reloaded.

Rohan strode on through the thicket without a glance at any of them. Then a flicker of gold and yellow caught his eye: he paused, turning to see a young woman posed beguilingly beneath a weeping willow. At her side one of his hunting dogs sprawled, its tail flopping back and forth as the young woman stroked its muzzle. Rohan stared at the woman, trying to place her; but then a soft explosion of wings came from a few yards off. Automatically he swiveled and discharged his weapon.

A clean miss. The grouse flew on. Rohan's gamekeeper clucked softly, shaking his head.

"A rare miss, Your Eminence."

Rohan looked back, annoyed, at the young woman beneath the willow. "You distracted me," he announced, stepping toward her.

Jeanne looked up as the Cardinal's shadow fell across the grass. "Then I have fulfilled my obligation as a woman," she replied coyly.

Rohan smiled, intrigued. Behind him one of his guards approached, but the Cardinal dismissed him with a wave. "I am unfamiliar with you, Madame," he said.

Jeanne dipped her head, a blush coloring her cheeks. "You are right to assume I have intruded. My curiosity about Your Eminence overcame my sense of decorum."

The Cardinal's smile broadened. "And what could ignite such curiosity?" he asked playfully.

Jeanne waited a moment, then looked up at him boldly. "I have heard it said that you are a man of copious desires."

Rohan stared at her appraisingly, then nodded slightly. "Some desires run deeper than others."

For another minute Rohan stood there, gazing at this provocative creature. At last he said, "You may visit me in my private salon in an hour's time. I will tell the servants to let you in."

He left, and Jeanne buried her face in the hound's fur to hide her smile.

Chapter

TEN

~❧ ❧~

When Jeanne arrived at Rohan's chambers she found him no longer in his hunting garb, but instead dressed in a sumptuous robe of violet silk and satin, tied with a gold-tasseled sash. They exchanged pleasantries, the usual round of verbal dueling that the Cardinal was accustomed to engaging in when he first met a woman of the aristocracy, as this fetching creature claimed she was. The claim itself could hardly be verified by her waving about her parchment scroll, but Rohan was not a snob in that strictest sense: when it came to women, he was a true democrat. The only hierarchy he acknowledged was that of female beauty, and in that, at least, the Comtesse was a genuine aristocrat.

"And now—shall we retire for a light repast?" The Cardinal beckoned her toward the door of his bedchamber, where he had ordered a dining table to be brought. "Some snails, perhaps, and champagne? L'ortolans?"

Jeanne lowered her eyes, smiling, then said, "Before we share such exquisite pleasures, I think I have something that might interest you, Your Eminence."

He stopped, surprised at this breach of seduction etiquette, and looked back at her. "And what could possibly interest me more than your own delightful self?"

"This."

Jeanne extended a kid-gloved hand toward him. In it was a thick envelope, with the Royal Coat of Arms embossed upon the crimson wax seal. Rohan hesitated. Then he strode toward her, took the letter, opened it and read.

"I companion the Queen most days at Versailles," Jeanne explained in a casual tone, pacing the length of Rohan's salon. "These are letters that she has written to me, during my time abroad."

The Cardinal finished reading. For some time he stood by the window, gazing at the signature on the bottom of the thick creamy paper, flowing violet ink letters in a carefree script.

Antoinette de France

He tapped the letter against his hand. Behind

him, a door opened and his secretary, Abel Duphot, entered. Rohan nodded absently as Duphot crossed to his desk and began doing clerical work. After a moment Rohan turned and walked back to where Jeanne stood, showing great interest in a vase full of silk flowers. He dropped the letter on the table next to the vase. A small stack of other letters stood there; he stared at them, then at Jeanne.

"Why bring these to my attention?"

Jeanne met his gaze. "The damaged feelings between you and Antoinette are well known. But old wounds may be healing."

Rohan fought to keep his tone even. "The Queen has said as much?"

Jeanne hesitated. "It is intuition on my part, I confess. But I feel that with . . . subtle persuasion . . . you could make progress with Her Majesty."

Rohan's gaze sharpened. "And you will apply these gentle pressures in return for—what?"

"Your Eminence's grace is all I require," replied Jeanne demurely.

The Cardinal waited, knowing there was more.

"And—" Jeanne raised her eyes shyly. "Your patronage, from time to time."

Rohan nodded: this, at last, was a language he could comprehend. He stepped over to a settee plumped with red velvet cushions and reclined upon it. An embroidered slipper dangled from his foot as he studied Jeanne with all the subtlety and charity of a viper preparing to strike.

"Your offer is compelling." At Jeanne's delighted smile he held out a warning hand. "Yet, I must decline. You are most likely a fraud. The court is riddled with them, and a man of my office is often a target."

Jeanne stared at him, her eyes brimming with injured pride and dismay. "That you should doubt my truthfulness is indeed a hurtful blow."

"Regardless of the state of your truthfulness, Countess, you do not lack tenacity—"

He licked his lips. "—and *that* I find exciting."

Jeanne slipped a lace handkerchief from her dress and dabbed at her eye. The Cardinal stood, glancing to where his secretary sifted through a heap of parchments. "Ah, now I have upset you. Abel, leave us. I wish to offer the Countess a word of comfort in private."

Abel smiled knowingly. He gathered the parchments, bowed, and closed the painted doors of the Cardinal's chamber as he left. Rohan walked to a side table where a crystal decanter and two glasses were set. He filled a glass and offered it to Jeanne.

"I was wrong to come here." Jeanne looked around uneasily. For the first time she felt exposed, vulnerable; as completely out of her element as she had ever been. "I—I see that now."

"Yet you are here." Rohan offered the glass of wine. She shook her head and took a few steps away. The Cardinal smiled, and downed the glass in one swallow. "And since you are here," he went on silkily, "we should make the effort to know one another unfettered by outside disturbances."

Jeanne stopped in front of the window, staring out to where the members of the Cardinal's hunting party still laughed and gossiped beneath brightly colored linen tents. When she finally spoke, it was with difficulty: it took all her will to maintain the tone of confidence she needed, else all was lost.

"I cannot be comfortable in the presence of a man who doubts me." Rohan could not see how her hands trembled as she twisted the silk handkerchief between damp fingers.

"In times of doubt," Rohan countered with the smallest of smiles, "prayer is the answer."

Jeanne turned back to him. Casually he tossed one of the red velvet pillows onto the floor before him, then stared at her commandingly. "Kneel before me. Kneel, and I will rest my hands upon your shoulders, and we will pray together."

Jeanne shook her head forcefully. "I respectfully decline, Your Eminence."

Rohan's eyes gleamed; this was the part of the hunt he loved: his prey showing fear, feigned or real, but his prey within his grasp all the same. Slowly he stepped toward Jeanne, and took her hands in his. "I am the Cardinal of all France, Countess. If the Cardinal wishes you to pray with him, why then you will do so."

Alarm flared in Jeanne's face as he pulled her to him, his silk gown rustling as he began to kiss the warm skin along the smooth curve of her neck. "You will not hold back," he murmured. "You will pray deeply, and with great conviction—"

He started to force her to her knees. Jeanne tried to resist, pushing at him, when suddenly he grabbed her wrist and pulled her to her feet.

"Where did you get this?" he demanded, pointing at the silk handkerchief still in her hand. On one corner, in tiny stitches, was embroidered Antoinette's crest and initials.

"Antoinette's chambers," said Jeanne haltingly. "She—she does the embroidery herself."

The Cardinal stared at her for a long time.

Finally, "I've noticed them," he said brusquely. "They are rather unique."

"I saw no harm."

Before he could stop her, she turned and walked quickly to the table, retrieving her letters and laying the handkerchief in their place.

"A reminder of what might have been," she said, giving him a swift look and then hurrying to the door. Rohan remained by the table, picking up the handkerchief and letting its silken folds slide across his fingertips.

"Perhaps—perhaps there is a way," he said at last. He drew the handkerchief to his throat and touched it to a jeweled crucifix nestled there. "A means by which we can verify your claim to a title . . ."

Chapter

ELEVEN

Yet before he could consider assisting the young Comtesse de La Motte, Rohan had to determine that she was not a spy sent by the court, or worse, an impostor whose wiles had been paid for by a cuckolded husband, or even (God forbid!) another high-ranking member of Mother Church. To this end, the Cardinal arranged for the Comtesse to accompany him that night, to a most secret and unusual assignation.

"I have taken under my patronage the most extraordinary man."

Inside Rohan's elaborate black japanned coach, the Comtesse sat and tried not to appear unduly impressed by the Cardinal's words. "He is the Grand Cophta of the Secret Order of Masons," the Cardinal went on in a conspiratorial tone. "Grandmaster of the Illuminati, the German mystic elite."

They had arrived at the House of Rohan. The Cardinal stepped out first, extending an arm for Jeanne to clasp as she followed him, past ranks of scarlet-clad guards and into the château. "He is an accomplished alchemist and somnambulist."

Rohan halted in front of a long corridor, and brusquely dismissed the last of his guards. He took a key from beneath his cape and unlocked a small side door, which opened onto a narrow, twisting passage, lit by guttering candles set in iron holders. "This way," said Rohan.

He stepped in front of Jeanne, removing a taper and holding it up to light their way. "We are entering the Rohan family's catacombs—please be careful as you walk. I don't wish to add another corpse to those already sleeping here."

Jeanne shuddered, drawing her cloak about her, and followed close upon the Cardinal's heels. "This man claims to have conquered disease and death several times over," the Cardinal continued, as calmly as though they still sat within his coach. "Many believe him to be no less than three thousand years old."

Before them the passage widened. A set of immense oaken doors, bound with iron hinges, stood half-open. Beyond them Jeanne could glimpse the welcome glow of candlelight. "If anyone can know that your overtures are authentic," the Cardinal finished, sweeping through the doors, "it will be him."

They were inside an echoing, cathedral-like space. Vaulted ceilings arched high overhead; a chandelier, unlit, depended from the vault. An altar at the far end of the vast space was arranged with numerous skulls, suggesting another sort of Mass than those at which the Cardinal usually presided. Guards in the Cardinal's crimson livery stood at attention near a long table aglow with thick beeswax candles that softened the room with their fragrance. Rohan gestured for Jeanne to take her place there, among the twenty guests already seated. She did so, trying not to look out of place—she recognized several Comtes and Comtesses, a Baron, and any number of intimates from the court.

"I welcome you all," the Cardinal announced as he strode to the head of the table. "And I will welcome now our most honored guest—"

Rohan stood before his chair and inclined his head. Another figure stepped from the shadows. A man, almost supernaturally tall, wearing a floor-length cape of blue fox furs. He had a smooth high forehead, crowned by a shock of black upswept hair, a neatly trimmed beard and dandyish waxed mustache.

But there was nothing remotely foppish about Giuseppe Balsamo, who called himself the Comte de Cagliostro. A famed magician and hypnotist, he claimed to possess untold powers, including necromancy—powers that would eventually lead to him being brought before the Inquisition and imprisoned as a sorcerer and heretic. Now, however, Cagliostro counted the Cardinal de Rohan among his friends and protectors. He stepped with exaggerated slowness to the end of the table opposite Rohan, finally halting and turning to face the Cardinal's guests.

A cry escaped from one of the women: the eyes that Cagliostro turned upon them possessed neither iris nor pupil. Two dull-white orbs, glowing spectrally in the candlelight, passed their empty gaze over each of the guests. The woman who first exclaimed grabbed the table edge, half-standing, then dropped to the floor in a faint. Cagliostro looked away, unconcerned, and shrugged off his blue fox cape, revealing an indigo robe thickly embroidered with strange symbols—Cabalistic figures and the rune-like designs favored by the Order of Masons. Then he turned back to the guests, his blank eyes slowly rotating downward to display a pair of vivid ice-blue irises. At the table's far end, Cardinal Rohan raised both his hands in greeting.

"Count Cagliostro, we are honored."

Cagliostro walked the length of the table, ignoring the Cardinal's introduction. He paused to lift a heavy candle from its gold sconce and hold it before his face.

"When I was a boy," he began in velvety, caressing tones, "I journeyed into the desert. The Egyptian landscape was quite flat at that time, for the pyramids had not yet been built."

As he spoke, the candle flame began to burn higher and higher. Jeanne craned her neck to get a better view of the magician, as Cagliostro continued, pacing slowly around the table as he spoke.

"In that wilderness I was captured by barbaric priests whose order subsisted on human blood."

Gasps came from the assembled guests; Cagliostro's candle flared like a torch. Jeanne felt her mouth go dry; she fought her fear at the thought of being somehow discovered by this man. She glanced at the Cardinal beside her. He was staring raptly at Cagliostro, who continued to hold the room mesmerized with his seductive voice.

"It was there that I was bestowed with the power of entering trances, in which state I commune freely with an angel of light and an angel of darkness. It is from these two sources that I draw my prognostications."

Jeanne leaned over and whispered to Rohan defensively, "This man is a charlatan. I will not be judged by him."

The Cardinal gave her a warning look. "I keep an open mind, Countess. I suggest you do the same."

As they spoke, Cagliostro was making his way among the seated guests. When he reached Jeanne's chair he paused, his icy blue gaze falling upon her.

She looked back, praying that her unease did not show. Cagliostro only smiled—knowingly, as though the two of them shared a history that he knew by heart. Then he took another step, and halted behind the elegantly dressed gentleman seated to her right.

"Were you aware, Count Greveck, that you have the pox?"

The Count turned to stare at him, openmouthed. Around the table the Cardinal's guests gasped and pushed their chairs away. Cagliostro smiled very slightly to himself. He had just started to turn toward another guest when he stopped, slowly turned and stared back at Jeanne.

"I am drawn to a new face," he said with cool charm. "So beautiful . . . I sense a woman of strong character. Very independent."

Jeanne smiled nervously, then said with a hint of flirtation, "For an Egyptian, you carry a decidedly Italian accent."

Cagliostro locked eyes with her.

"The Northern provinces, I'd speculate," she added, dipping her head demurely. At her side, Cardinal Rohan observed with keen interest as Cagliostro strode up to her chair.

"You have a refined ear," Cagliostro concurred, and inclined his head to her. "You have spent time in that ancient country?"

Jeanne nodded. "Yes."

"As have I. Centuries, all told. So forgive me if I

retain some of the Italian region's earthy tones, beautiful lady."

"You honor me, Monsieur," said Jeanne.

"I honor no one," Cagliostro said sharply. His gaze grew more intent, less friendly. "I merely speak of what I see. You have come to the Cardinal with an alliance, yes?"

Jeanne froze, knowing she had been discovered by this man—whoever he really was. She said cautiously, "I am certain that many people bring favorable offers before his Eminence."

"But yours is the one that concerns us this night—" Cagliostro said with a glow of triumph. "—Countess de La Motte."

At the sound of her proper title, Jeanne turned to Cardinal Rohan. He shook his head.

"I have not spoken a word about you to this man," he said. "He is truly a marvel."

Jeanne's searching eyes caught a glimpse of Abel standing in a corner of the room. "Or particularly well informed," she said in a low voice.

"Count Cagliostro has proven himself to me time and again." Rohan stared at her coldly. "I cannot say the same for you, Countess."

Cagliostro flicked a hand at her, as though ridding himself of a gnat. "Do you doubt my abilities, Countess?"

Jeanne stared at him uncomfortably, and Cagliostro shook his head. "There is much turmoil within you," he murmured. "And I sense fear as well."

The Cardinal looked at Cagliostro, then Jeanne. She struggled to appear calm, forcing a smile as she said, "I am not afraid. In fact, this is one of the more delightful evenings I've ever spent in a catacomb."

Chuckles echoed from around the table. Rohan frowned and placed a hand on Jeanne's arm, as Cagliostro silenced the others with a look, then brought his gaze back to Jeanne.

"Countess. You learned early on to mask what you were feeling. You've suffered great losses in your life. Irreplaceable losses." He paused, then asked, "Should I go deeper still?"

Jeanne chose her reply carefully. "I doubt there is a person in this room who has not lost something, or someone, that they feel cannot be replaced."

"You were taken in by strangers." Cagliostro's eyes narrowed; he spoke as though he and Jeanne were alone in the chamber. "You lived among wealth that was not your own. Always you were on the outside looking in. Longing for what was taken from you."

Jeanne stared at him in disbelief. *How could he know?* Her lips parted, wanting to command him to stop; but she said nothing. With a small smile Cagliostro stepped closer to her.

"But that was not what hurt the most." His voice dropped. "Shall I look deeper still?"

Jeanne said nothing. At her side the Cardinal watched her with cruel pleasure, as though she were a rabbit caught in a snare.

"I see you hovering over a cold grave," whispered Cagliostro. "Wishing it were your own. But it wasn't, was it, Countess?"

Jeanne blinked, tears welling in her eyes. She shook her head, begging him not to go on. Cagliostro ignored her. "A grave dug for a small coffin," he said. "Have I gone far enough?"

Indeed, it seemed he had. Without knowing where the strength came from, Jeanne stood. When she spoke her voice was composed.

"If I had doubts that you possess a gift, I was wrong. Intimidation is an old art form, Count Cagliostro. But no doubt you were there at its inception."

Caglisotro only continued to stare at her, unmoved and unimpressed.

Jeanne looked at the Cardinal. He sat gazing at Cagliostro smugly, supremely satisfied with the evening's entertainment thus far.

Drawing herself up, Jeanne gave him a small bow, turned and left the chamber. Cagliostro watched her go, then swiveled to face the remaining guests.

"Well then—who's next?" he asked puckishly.

But a few hours later, when he was alone with Rohan in the foyer of the House of Rohan, the Count was not so sanguine.

"The dark angel knows that one well," he said. "But I would not dismiss her entirely."

Cardinal Rohan nodded. "You called her an adventuress."

"Because she is proud." Cagliostro turned his piercing stare upon the Cardinal. "I sense an opportunity for Your Eminence, though how it will manifest itself is unclear to me at the present."

Rohan nodded thoughtfully, and for a long time afterward pondered the sorcerer's words.

Chapter

T W E L V E

O utside the Chapelle de Versailles, an intricate web of wood and rope and canvas had been erected: a scaffold that His Majesty the King himself had helped construct. Workmen were busy with smearing mortar onto the cracks in the chapel walls; they were grateful that this task, at least, the King chose not to "assist" with. It was difficult enough being a laborer in the court of Louis XVI; having to bite one's tongue while the clumsy Louis tripped over pilings and bales of hempen rope only made it that much worse.

"Smooth and even, Messieurs!" The King called out encouragement, as he paced atop the highest tier of scaffolding. "A job done with conscientiousness is a job that endures."

The masons exchanged looks. Only months before the King had nearly perished while "assisting" in a similar manner—only the quick reflexes of one of his laborers had kept him from walking off another scaffold and tumbling to his death. The worker had been rewarded with a pension, but Louis's passion for manual labor, unfortunately, had not been exhausted.

"If he directed government the way he directs a trowel, France would rule the world."

Several stories below, Louis's wife gazed fondly up at him. In her arms was one of her beloved little lapdogs, squirming and yipping imperiously; at her side walked Minister Breteuil. He glanced up at the King, then smiled guardedly at Antoinette.

"Well said, Your Majesty."

He followed her as with mincing steps she took a winding path that led away from the palace and into Versailles' formal gardens. Antoinette's chambermaid, Colleen, walked very slowly and at a respectful distance behind Her Majesty, ready to be at her side should she be commanded. The young Dauphin and Princess Royal were in more of a hurry: they flashed past, in pursuit of a brightly-colored box kite that the Dauphin was navigating among the topiary trees and hedges. The children's harried nursemaid dashed after them, her skirts held high as she made a rushed curtsey to the Queen.

Antoinette smiled after them. "They are such a comfort to me."

She turned to Breteuil then, her smile fading. "A wonderful—distraction." Her tone suddenly grew serious. "I have heard that there were more disturbances in the market district."

Minister Breteuil hesitated. "It was a small gathering of malcontents."

"How small of a gathering, House Minister?"

Breteuil did not hide his concern. "Nearly two hundred."

"And no doubt my name was used in vain."

"Arrests were made, naturally."

Antoinette shook her head. "You can silence their tongues, Breteuil, but never their thoughts."

She stopped, trailing a finger along a hawthorn branch. Her lapdog went into paroxysms of shrill barks. After a moment, Antoinette looked up at her House Minister. Her face was twisted with emotion. "Why do the people regard me with such hate? It wasn't always so."

"Your Majesty is not the source of their animosity," Breteuil replied with a trace of tenderness in his voice. "You are merely a symbol for them to aim at. Their minds are clouded by ideas of reform, force-fed to them by misguided extremists."

"This chasm of mistrust is unnecessary," said Antoinette sadly. "Am I so different from them? Are my children so different from their children?"

As she spoke, she gazed to where the young

Dauphin and Princess Royal stood at the base of a manicured boxtree hedge. Atop the pruned greenery, the Dauphin's kite hung precariously from a small protruding branch.

"Look what you've done!" the Princess Royal cried peevishly. "Our kite is lost!"

"You there!" cried the Dauphin, pointing at a courtier who stood nearby, gossiping with his cronies. "Assist me! Get on your knees—be quick about it!"

The courtier looked stunned. "But Monsieur Dauphin—"

"Are you a simpleton? I have given you a command!"

With an embarrassed glance at House Minister Breteuil, the courtier got down on all fours so that the Dauphin could clamber on his back and retrieve his plaything. Breteuil cleared his throat and looked away. Antoinette's dog began to grunt noisily, its tiny legs scrabbling at her bodice; Antoinette looked down, then turned and cried in a shrill voice, "Colleen! Stop dawdling! Come now, see to Precious's needs—be quick about it!"

The chambermaid hurried to her side, and the Queen shoved the little dog at her. "My angel wishes to relieve herself—take her, you dim girl!"

"Yes, Your Majesty."

The chambermaid stood, the yipping dog thrashing in her arms. As Antoinette walked off, a monogrammed handkerchief fluttered unseen from her reticule. Colleen looked around quickly and stooped to retrieve it, then, cursing beneath her breath at the repellent little lapdog, hastened her away on the Queen's business.

～ JEANNE HAD TO GIVE HIS FOOTMAN A GOLD coin to gain entrance to Count Cagliostro's chamber: if a sorcerer's wooden staff could not easily be broken, still his household staff could be bribed. She smiled at the knowledge, but her smile faded as she entered the Count's chamber.

A blue haze of incense hung throughout the room, pierced here and there by murky orange candle flames and smoking joss sticks. An immense dressing table stood before an ormolu mirror, man-high, surrounded by wooden mannequin heads fitted with all manner of wigs. The effect was not reassuring: it brought to mind Monsieur Guillotin's recent invention, and Jeanne quickly looked away. Elsewhere cloaks festooned with cabalistic symbols hung from the wall, and banners embroidered with runic designs. There was no sign of Cagliostro.

"You show incredible audacity in seeking me." Jeanne gasped as a figure moved suddenly from the shadows: the Count, clad in a crimson silk dressing gown. "Even though I knew that you would."

Jeanne shook her hair back defiantly. "Did you denounce me to the Cardinal?" Behind her came the sound of a door opening. She glanced back to see a servant in turban and violet pantaloons, his face respectfully downcast as he carried a gold goblet to his master. Cagliostro took the drink, giving the servant a sharp look. The man left; Cagliostro set the goblet upon a small table, and once more turned his hooded eyes upon Jeanne.

"I told the Cardinal that, despite your troubled past, I did sense an opportunity."

Jeanne let this sink in. Then, "You left the door open for me," she said slowly.

"And I can close it just as quickly. If you want my visions of you to remain positive, I will in return demand a share in whatever you gain from the Cardinal."

Jeanne was silent. Finally she said, "I admit that I was caught off guard by the intimate details you knew about my life. And then I realized—the Marquise Boullainvillers."

Cagliostro turned from her with supreme indifference, but Jeanne went on. "A charitable woman who took me in—as you well know. But she was also superstitious. Magicians and mesmerists often entertained in her parlor."

"What has that got to do with me?"

"A person of your colorful nature might well have found his way into her home. In the course of your—prognostications—you may have asked her a few questions."

Cagliostro whirled to glare at her, his deep-set eyes ominously aglow.

"You're guessing, Countess. Grabbing at straws."

"I need only raise doubts. In your case—" She lifted her head and met his gaze. "A little suspicion could go a long way."

With a roar Cagliostro tore his wig from his skull and flung it upon the floor. When he spoke it was in unaccented French, coarse and furious.

"If you wish to trade secrets in front of the Cardinal, Countess, remember that *I* have his confidence."

Abruptly he lunged at her, enraged. "And the court is filled with hungry minds who will eagerly tear you apart if I feed them enough lies! Go against me and *I will destroy you*!"

Jeanne took a swift step backward and stared at him, unafraid. "That is precisely why I will do it. *I* have nothing to lose."

Cagliostro froze. After a moment he spun on his heel and crossed the room, sinking into a chair.

Jeanne watched him, then said, "Keep the Cardinal interested in me and you will share in the rewards. But if you get greedy, Count, remember that our fates are now joined as one."

For several minutes Cagliostro sat, brooding. At last he picked up the goblet where it stood on the table beside him, downed its contents, and sighed. He said no more; but Jeanne knew better than to press him further. With a small smile she turned and left the chamber, knowing that, in his silence, she had received all the answers she desired.

❧ IT WAS DARK WHEN SHE LEFT CAGLIOSTRO'S quarters, but she had yet another assignation in the city that night. She found Retaux where they had earlier agreed to meet, in a shadowed alley near a noisy tavern. He greeted her silently, raising his lantern so that its wan gleam fell across her hooded face; then motioned for her to follow him.

They made their way through a maze of passageways and narrow back streets choked with refuse and half-starved feral dogs that snarled, then slunk off at their approach. At last they came to an arched passage that opened out beneath an ancient bridge. Above them crumbling stonework was laced with moss and ropes of dead vines. Below the river flowed, dark and viscous as oil, casting back cloudy images of bridge, sky, stone.

"Such secrecy, Retaux?" Jeanne asked with mocking distaste. She pulled aside her cloak to keep it from snagging on a heap of fallen stones, slick with damp and rot.

"Patience, Madame," he retorted, and indicated the river. "I have been very busy on your behalf."

Jeanne looked where he pointed. At the water's edge a figure waited. Slight, with a piquant face visible even in the darkness, her hands working nervously beneath the shawl she clutched to her breast. As Jeanne and Retaux approached she cried out softly, startled, then walked quickly toward them. Retaux raised his lantern so that its light fell upon her face, and turned to Jeanne.

"Countess, allow me to introduce Colleen. This lovely young lady is a maidservant in the Queen's private rooms."

Jeanne gazed at the girl with sudden understanding—and admiration for Retaux. Colleen smiled at him shyly, and in a sweet fluting voice said, "I have come just as you requested, Monsieur."

"And I, too, am pleased, my dear." Retaux returned her smile as Jeanne fought a stab of jealousy: what charms! He could seduce the Queen herself, if he chose! But Retaux only continued smoothly. "Now show the Countess what you have for her."

From beneath her shawl Colleen withdrew several sheets of thick creamy stationery. Each was embossed with the Queen's coat of arms. Before Jeanne could so much as gasp in amazement, the young girl reached into her pocket to display a white silk handkerchief embroidered in crimson silk with Antoinette's initials.

"Is she not a treasure?" murmured Retaux.

Colleen looked over her shoulder, her smile flickering to unease. "They would cut off my hands if I were caught taking these," she said. Then her gaze drifted upward to Retaux. Her mouth softened.

"But Monsieur de Vilette was so heartfelt in his request—I could not refuse him."

Retaux smiled modestly as Jeanne raised an eyebrow. "You *have* been busy on my behalf." She turned, unfastening a brooch from beneath her cloak and placing it into Colleen's hand. "There—I haven't much to give you now, but there will be more later. I promise . . . "

Colleen stared at the brooch in her open palm. After a minute Retaux reached over and placed a few coins beside it, then gently closed her fingers over them. With a nod, Colleen handed the stationery and the handkerchief to Jeanne.

"If this means trouble for that Austrian bitch," the Queen's chambermaid said with a wicked little grin, "then that alone will suffice."

Whatever he may have secretly felt about Cagliostro's claims, or Jeanne de La Motte's accusations against him, Rohan was only too pleased to entertain the visiting Comte with the Cardinal's customary extravagance and élan.

For Rohan, this meant a private orgy—by invitation only, such invitations being highly sought after by members of the court's inner circle. The furtive nature of the goings-on, heightened by the aura of scandal and forbidden fruit (always the sweetest and hardest to obtain) that accrued to the Cardinal's religious rank; the number and quality of the young women, very occasionally and by special request accompanied by very young men and gynanders: all of these things conspired to make such gatherings at the House of Rohan the stuff of legend.

With the sorcerer Cagliostro there, of course, an orgy could also become the stuff of legerdemain. For the occasion, Cagliostro wore his formal black satin cape and high black boots, but otherwise eschewed the costumes favored by the Cardinal's twenty other gentlemen guests. The invitation had read *To the Seraglio*, and a secret chamber, for many years a private lair of the Rohan men wherein they entertained their mistresses and catamites, had for the occasion been transformed into a Turkish harem. Huge velvet pillows were everywhere, and the very low seats called ottomans, as well as lush carpets and hangings from Persia and the Orient. The women too wore exotic garb—ballooning trousers of crimson and yellow silk, or skirts cropped high to display *caches des sexes* filigreed with jewels, or flimsy veils of cobweb silk that enhanced rather than hid the beauty of the wearer. The Cardinal's guests were scattered throughout the seraglio, the men playing games of chance—faro, tunk—the women toying with the men, or each other, in an effort to rouse the jaded appetites of aristocrats and ambassadors.

"It is a successful evening, *non*?" The Cardinal was perched on the edge of an immense mahogany chair that had once graced a medieval church in Rome. A silver-bodied opium pipe rested upon his long fingers; now and then he drew from it luxuriously, the sweet smoke mingling with the scents of civet and sex that filled the room.

Cagliostro leaned upon a pillow on the floor. To either side of him twin beauties, dark-haired Gemini with powdered faces and lips bruised from kissing, sat and played with the bejeweled gussets of his jacket. Cagliostro opened his mouth and sent a burst of smoke into the face of one of the women. With a sigh she sank, heavy-lidded, back onto the pillow.

"In my experience," Cagliostro said, with a lascivious glance at the smiling Cardinal, "the ancient Queen Bathsheba had no equal when it came to the art of love."

He ran a finger along the collarbone of the woman beside him. "She had the eyes of a hungry jaguar, rosy breasts begging to be touched, and a tempting, oh-so-gifted mouth."

From a golden perch behind him came the low cooing song of a quartet of tame lovebirds, their bright feathers muted in the smoke. With a smile Cagliostro leaned back, took one of the fluttering birds into his big hand, and turned to the woman. Without warning he closed his hand on the little creature, seeming to crush it.

"Ah, no!" the woman cried, her voice soft and melancholy as the bird's. Then, slowly as a blossom unfolding, Cagliostro opened his hand. Where the lovebird had been was a glittering golden pendant in the shape of a bird. With a flourish, he turned and presented the lovely trinket to one of the twins.

Rohan chuckled. "It took our Lord seven days to create the world," he said, shaking his head in amazement. "I wonder how long it would take you, my friend."

From across the room came the muffled gasp of a woman in the throes of climax. Rohan glanced aside, and saw Abel Duphot approaching him.

"Your Eminence," his secretary whispered. "The Countess de La Motte is here and has asked to see you. She says it is of the greatest importance, and that you would welcome her news."

With a quick look back at Cagliostro, now in the embrace of both twins, Rohan stood and left. Hidden behind a tapestry was a small door; he ducked into this, and within minutes was in his own private salon.

"Your Eminence." The Comtesse turned and curtsied. With no further greeting or explanation she handed him an envelope. The Cardinal took it, suppressing emotion at sight of the familiar gilt-edged stationery inside. He scanned it, then looked at Jeanne and read aloud.

"'An apology would seem the proper starting point if we are to mend damaged feelings.'"

He stopped, and tapped the letter against his hand. "A Prince of the House of Rohan apologize? It has never been done."

"For years you have anguished because Antoinette has not given you a look or a word. You now hold in your hand a letter from her of the most affable nature."

For a long time the Cardinal was silent. Finally he said, "I will admit that Antoinette's loathing of me has become more than an—an irritation."

"You need not suffer anymore . . . as long as my considerations are met."

Rohan spun and began to pace about the room. "If I were to acquiesce, would the reply be delivered by your own hand?"

"It would reach Her Majesty no other way."

Rohan stopped and looked at her, then nodded. "A notice of credit shall be advanced to you for the sum of, shall we say—five thousand gold Louis."

Jeanne lifted her chin. "Twenty thousand would seem more appropriate. For now."

Rohan smiled. "Are you attempting to bargain with me?"

"I merely seek compensation equal to the rare opportunity which I offer to you."

The Cardinal's smile evaporated as he crossed the room toward her. "Countess de La Motte . . . not so long ago, a young woman much like yourself attempted to extort money from me. She came forth with claims of having experienced some mistreatment at my hands. Her accusations, of course, were unfounded."

He circled Jeanne as he spoke, and then walked behind her. "She was the niece of the Captain of my private guards," he said softly, resting his hands lightly on her hips. "One night, her uncle slipped into this young woman's room with a very sharp blade."

He reached around her, his hand touching her on the stomach and lingering there. Jeanne froze, her breath coming fast and shallow, but did not move. Very slowly Rohan ran his finger from the soft swell of her belly, between her breasts and finally to her neck. "He slit the poor girl from her genitalia to the dimple on her pretty chin. Now—"

He brought his face close to hers, his lips brushing her ear as he whispered, "Do you know why a man would do such a thing to his own kin?"

Jeanne swallowed, shook her head. Rohan kissed her earlobe and murmured, *"Because I told him to."*

Jeanne made a small sound in her throat and tried to move away, but the Cardinal's grip only tightened. *"Never* test my good nature, Countess," he warned her.

Once again Jeanne pulled away. This time, he let her go. In a frightened rush she headed for the door, abruptly stopped and straightened, gathering her courage before turning back to Rohan.

"I must ask that Your Eminence be mindful," she said, praying her voice not betray her. "I can shatter this fragile correspondence as easily as I formed it."

The Cardinal surveyed her through slitted eyes. "As your situation improves," he said, his voice taut and threatening as a trip wire, "mine had better do the same."

For another moment Jeanne stood there, her hand cold upon his chamber door. Then she turned and fled.

Chapter

FOURTEEN

❧❦

I t did not take long for Jeanne to make good use
of the Cardinal's gold Louis. There were visits to
furniture-makers and weavers of tapestries, an afternoon spent in the warm, mint-scented shopfront
of a carpet-dealer from Istanbul; luxurious morn-
ings of sifting through bolts of silk damask and lace
and satin and brocade, employing dressmakers and
needleworkers and milliners. At the end of three
weeks, both Jeanne de La Motte and her apartments had been transformed, the former into a
breathing simulacrum of elegance, with enough
vanity to pique the continuing interest of young
men; the latter into a grand salon befitting one in-

volved in an intimate correspondence with the Queen.

It was this last which occupied Jeanne one late afternoon. She was wearing her most recent acquisition, a gorgeous pearl-embroidered dressing gown that set off her black hair and pale skin, the faint blush of crimson on her cheeks. In the center of her salon was a gilded statue of an angel, after the Italian Michelangelo; Jeanne walked slowly around this, seeming to think aloud, while at a small neatly-appointed writing desk the dashing Retaux de Vilette sat, a long swan's-quill pen quivering in his hand.

"'My dearest Cardinal.'" Jeanne let her hand rest upon the angel's head and gazed pensively out the window. "'I have received your solicitations for a personal audience and will give your request the utmost consideration.'"

Retaux's hand moved across the gilt-edged page, a beautifully-formed stream of words flowing in its wake. He paused to adjust his own dressing gown, heavy black and gold silk jacquard, no pearls; and glanced up, a small smile tugging at his lips as he watched his mistress at work.

"'Your apologies for past discretions, though . . .'" Jeanne hesitated, frowning.

"Bounteous?" prodded Retaux helpfully.

"'Bounteous in nature, are no longer necessary.'"

With exaggerated courtliness, Jeanne walked until she stood behind him, and playfully bent to kiss the nape of his neck. "'Jeanne de La Motte informs me of your changed attitudes and behavior,'" she recited in a teasing tone. "'My dearest Jeanne, whom each day I find a more and more . . . '"

"Succulent?" Retaux grasped one of her hands and kissed it. "Tasty?"

"' . . . *capable* friend. In time, Cardinal, your request for a private meeting will be taken *in hand*.'"

As she uttered these last words Retaux reached to cup her breast in his palm. Jeanne laughed, and gently placed his hand back upon the desk.

"'Until then,'" Retaux said, pretending to groan, "'I must remain cautious.'"

With an impish grin, Jeanne leaned forward, sliding her hand beneath the folds of Retaux's robe and fondling him. He struggled to maintain composure as she continued.

"'There are those who could misconstrue such a meeting and do us both public harm. I look forward to your next correspondence. Always I remain, your devoted Sovereign—'"

Retaux swept the quill pen across the bottom of the page with a flourish.

"'Antoinette of France,'" he sang out triumphantly. He threw the quill aside and pulled Jeanne into his lap, tickling her and covering her face, her hands, her breasts with kisses.

"Madame!" The salon door flew open. Jeanne's

new maidservant, Rosalie, rushed into the room, pausing to curtsey to Retaux. "Madame must hurry! Her coiffure alone will take two hours!"

Retaux nodded. "Rosalie, I would like a moment with the Countess before I give her over to the world."

Rosalie curtsied again. "Yes, Monsieur," she said, and returned to the bedchamber. After she left Jeanne crossed to a sidetable where wine had been decanted into a crystal bottle. She poured herself a glass, took a sip and offered it to Retaux. He took it and drank thoughtfully.

"In the beginning," Jeanne said, tilting her head, "it was my intent to simply use you."

Retaux raised an eyebrow. "A confession? This is a fragile moment."

She touched a finger to his lips, silencing him. "And yet somewhere along the journey I have come to rely on you. I have never felt that way about anyone."

"I feel the same, Countess." His mouth brushed her cheek, then her chin, as she gazed at him uncertainly. "And it frightens me a little. But it does not frighten me enough—"

He kissed her then, one hand moving to untie the soft furls of her dressing gown; and in the moments that followed all uncertainty was gone.

Chapter

FIFTEEN

The Royal Opera was always where Paris society went to be seen, to gossip, to carry out
assignations and resolve rivalries; even, occasionally,
to watch the performance. Tonight courtiers had
gathered early, knowing that the Queen would be in
attendance. Those who lived or died by fashion had
made certain that their most exquisite finery was on
display. No one hoped, however—or dared—to
make as striking an impression as Antoinette in-
evitably would, when she made her entrance.

As always, her timing was impeccable—how
could it be otherwise? The opera could not begin
until Her Majesty appeared; nor could the rounds
of heightened talk and murmurs exchanged behind

fluttering fans or in the privacy of theater boxes. In the foyer of the Opera House, myriad courtiers waited, sharing whatever news they had acquired since last they met. These expectant moments formed the preprandial portion of the evening, conversational tidbits that whetted the appetite. Her Majesty's arrival, it went without saying, would comprise the main course.

A momentary silence like a gust of wind swept through the foyer. Automatically all eyes turned to gaze up at the magnificent curving staircase. For a heartbeat the space was empty, a stage waiting to be filled; and then Marie Antoinette appeared, flanked by Madame Campan and her six ladies-in-waiting. Pointedly delighted gasps and cries went up from those waiting and watching below, as Antoinette paused at the top of the staircase, to permit everyone the chance to see her new costume.

Clothing Her Majesty had almost become a blood sport of late: her desire for ever more extreme and novel confections in dress, makeup, and hair had made the fortune of any number of enterprising dressmakers and milliners, and exhausted or bankrupted countless others. Bankruptcy threatened members of the court as well: many aristocrats went into debt to finance their own wardrobes, buying wigs made of human hair at astronomical cost, rather than risk disapproval by wearing less expensive creations of horsehair.

And the horrors of millinery did not end there.

Far worse, many secretly thought, was actually having to *wear* the absurdly tall wigs that Antoinette favored. Twelve or eighteen inches worth of human hair, perched precariously atop a sort of horsehair pillow that might be another six inches in height, all of it anchored to one's own hair by steel pins long and sharp enough to draw blood. Real and wax fruit or blossoms, jewels, stuffed paroquets, flamingoes, or preserved butterflies might then be arranged within the coils and arabesques, and the whole obscene structure doused with a preserving pomade that, naturally, began to stink after a day or two. Because in order to recoup the sizable investment in time, design, and materials, of course one needs must *wear* the dreadful things for as long as was feasible (or fashionable).

Yet not even the most extraordinary hairpiece on display that night could match the creations debuted by Antoinette and her ladies-in-waiting. Nestled within the swirls of powdered hair were tiny gilded birdcages, lovely and delicate as music boxes; and nestled within the cages were tiny twittering canaries, fluttering scraps of sunlight that twittered and cheeped haplessly as the Queen and her coterie slowly descended the staircase.

"Ever the surprise, Your Majesty," one aristocratic dowager said, curtseying as Her Majesty passed. Antoinette smiled, nodding at the polite applause that greeted her when she reached the floor. Her courtiers had begun to gather around her, exclaiming over the captive birds, when abruptly the crowd's focus shifted, from Antoinette in the foyer to another figure standing at the top of the stairs.

It was Jeanne de La Motte. Her gown, simply but expensively tailored of damask silk and silver filigree, shimmered across her slender form like dark water. In place of one of the court's monstrous wigs she wore her own hair swept back from her face, the black curls setting off her unpowdered skin. A mist of taffeta surmounted by a few elegant plumes, a few artfully placed gardenias above her brow; and compared to Antoinette she was as fresh and ravishing as a girl at her first court masque.

The effect, needless to say, was not wasted upon those in the Royal Opera House.

"The gem of the evening," exclaimed Comte Blui-etu, one of Antoinette's intimates. Too late he realized the rashness of speaking his thoughts: a flashing glance from the Queen, and the Comte quickly made himself disappear within the crowd.

Others were slightly more discreet. A handful of young cavaliers made graceful *exeunts* to Her Majesty, then clustered about the Comtesse de La Motte, begging to carry her fan, her gloves, her heart. Jeanne smiled with studied shyness, her eyes downcast; and looked out to see a number of courtiers gazing at her. To a man and woman, each smiled and nodded at her approvingly. Jeanne turned back, casting her gaze toward the Queen, but Antoinette was already gone.

"The little bud has finally blossomed." A pair of dowagers, one of them the redoubtable Madame Pomfre, stood somewhat apart from the crowd watching Jeanne. Madame Pomfre's companion fanned herself and shook her head. "What could have brought about such a transformation?"

Madame Pomfre gazed across the room to where Retaux de Vilette stood talking animatedly with another group. "I've heard from a confidential source that Antoinette has taken the young Countess under her wing."

As she spoke she smiled. Sighting her, Retaux lifted his chin and smiled back.

And just behind Madame Pomfre the eavesdropping court jeweler, Bassenge, peered with growing interest past Madame's elaborate coiffure to where the fetching young Comtesse de La Motte stood within her little claque of admirers.

I t was in a celebratory mood that Jeanne and Retaux returned to her apartment late that night. There had been champagne at the opera, followed by champagne in the coach home. Now other pleasures awaited them. Laughing, Retaux grabbed Jeanne playfully around the waist and drew her to him.

"Her Majesty cannot command you here," he said. "But I can . . ."

He kissed her and she responded, feverishly, moaning softly as his hands sought the laces of her gown. The silken folds slid from her shoulders to the floor, the gardenias in her hair followed, as Jeanne struggled first with the maddening number of buttons on Retaux's waistcoat and then with the yards of ruffled fabric around his cuffs.

And still there was the final battleground to be traversed: Jeanne's corset, a lethal-looking armature of whalebone and steel and waxed linen. In frustration, Retaux yanked his dagger from its sheath and began slicing through the constricting hoops. After a moment he hesitated, looking up at Jeanne and wondering if, perhaps, he had gone too far.

Obviously he had not gone far enough: Jeanne grabbed the dagger and cut through the row of laces along the side, so that the corset fell away and she stood before him in only her chemise and silk stockings.

"There," she said in triumph.

She pulled him down, the damask gown and gardenias a fragrant bed as Retaux sprawled on his back and Jeanne straddled him, lifting her chemise. He pulled her closer, rolling until she was beneath him; then he entered her. Her breath quickened with his thrusts, and his gaze softened as he focused on her climax, and then his own.

"These moments are what I live for," he whispered minutes later. Gently he brushed the hair from her forehead, then kissed her brow. "It is the only time I feel that you are completely mine."

From the darkened room behind them came the clink of crystal, the sound of wine being poured into a glass.

"The Countess gives her heart sparingly," a deep voice intoned.

With a low cry Retaux leaped up, grabbing a heavy candlestick and brandishing it as he strained to find the intruder in the shadows. At the serving table near the window a lamp flared as someone turned up the wick. Its yellow glow illuminated the figure of a man, tall and black-haired, with an athlete's build beneath his military uniform. His dark eyes stared broodingly from a once-handsome face that now bore the fine lines and hollows of dissipation.

"Nicolas!" Jeanne sprang to her feet, flushed with anger. "How dare you? This is unforgivable!"

Nicolas de La Motte shrugged. "It is so seldom that a man has the opportunity to watch his wife make love from that exact vantage point."

"You are not welcome here," Jeanne retorted angrily, pulling on her dressing gown. "Go back to your actress."

Nicolas shook his head. "Ah, but *non*! Upon hearing of your change of fortune, my dear Jeanne, my affection for you rekindled. In a blink, my actress seemed drab and common. Whereas you, my dear—you were once again my reason to live. It was bound to happen, I suppose—"

With a shout Retaux lunged at him. Nicolas was on his feet in an eyeblink, sword drawn and slicing through the air as Retaux grabbed his chair and used it as a shield. Fragments of wood flew across the room as Nicolas backed Retaux into a corner. With his free hand he grabbed a crystal vase, tossing it into the air and catching it as he held Retaux at sword's-point a few feet off.

"No one would dispute your mastery at making something out of nothing, dear Jeanne," he said, continuing to keep Retaux at bay. "Yet this is, by far, your magnum opus."

Retaux looked around desperately, and saw his dagger on Jeanne's writing desk. His discarded shirt covered the blade. He tossed aside the chair and lunged for the desk; at the same instant Nicolas threw the vase. It shattered above Retaux's head, covering the floor with slivers of glass. Retaux's fingers grazed the hilt of his dagger, but before he could grasp it Nicolas had leaped forward and swiped his blade against Retaux's bare chest. Retaux staggered back, blood seeping from a shallow wound.

"Nicolas!" Jeanne shouted. "I beg you, do not do this!"

Her husband's blade flashed again: another shallow cut bloomed on Retaux's neck. "To what do you refer, my cherished?" Nicolas purred.

"I've known you a long time, Nicolas," Retaux broke in, his voice strong despite his wounds. "You are hot-tempered but not unreasonable. Let us sort this out in some other fashion."

Nicolas's dark eyes held the feral glint of madness. His sword moved with slow, hypnotic force as he followed his prey's slightest move. "What happened, Retaux?" he asked. "Did you grow weary of plowing your way through every old woman at court?"

Retaux backed away, laughing uneasily. He reached for another chair, then said, "If you had been present to begin with, I would not be here now. Did that thought ever cross your empty mind?"

With an enraged shout Nicolas lunged at him. Screaming, Jeanne propelled herself onto Nicolas's back, knocking him off balance. They fell, catching Retaux as they did, and then all three of them went flying backward against a window. Glass flew everywhere. Jeanne and Retaux tried to catch their breath, but before they could rise Nicolas was on his feet again, sword raised, advancing on Retaux with murder in his eyes.

Jeanne screamed. *"Nicolas, no!"*

And then an explosion ripped through the chamber. Nicolas's body whipped around, then fell to the floor with a crash. Jeanne blinked in astonishment. She tore her gaze from Nicolas to see a small figure standing in the doorway, blue smoke surrounding her like a halo.

"Madame, forgive me." It was Rosalie, her chambermaid, still in her nightclothes. In her trembling hand was Jeanne's tiny pistol. "I—I heard noises, and took the pistol from your bedside."

On the floor Nicolas lay, unmoving. "Rosalie!"

Jeanne started toward her. "Rosalie, you've just shot my husband!"

With a wail Rosalie dropped the pistol and burst into tears. "Oh, God in heaven! I have killed a man, and at my early age!"

Chapter

SEVENTEEN

~❧❧~

I t took nearly an hour for the surgeon to arrive. When he did, it was a more subdued and far less sinister-looking Nicolas who lay sprawled face-down on Jeanne's dining room table, his bloody trousers draped over a chair and his *derrière* exposed to Dr. Legear's ministrations.

"It was not my intent to hurt anyone. You know that!" Nicolas said in an injured tone. He took a swig from a bottle of brandy, then glared at Jeanne and Retaux.

"You were playing the bully, and you got the bully's due," his wife retorted, unimpressed. Nicolas howled with pain as Dr. Legear's metal probe dug deeper into his backside.

"Goddamn you, man! Are you digging for potatoes? Go easy!"

Dr. Legear glared at him, sweat dripping from his pale face. "I did not presume to tell you how to get this projectile where it is. Do not presume to tell me how to get it out." He took a pair of hooked metal tweezers and turned back to his work.

"Oh, God*∂amn*!" Nicolas shouted.

Rosalie entered the room, glanced at Nicolas, and gave him a wide berth. "Countess," she said, handing Jeanne a card. "A gentleman is here to see you."

"Send him away!" yelled Nicolas. "This is obviously an inconvenient time!"

Jeanne studied the card and shot Nicolas a disdainful look. "Attend to your business with Dr. Legear, and leave me to attend with mine."

She handed the card to Retaux, who read it with growing interest, then turned to Rosalie. "Tell Monsieur Bassenge I will be with him momentarily."

"Yes, Countess." The chambermaid curtsied and left. Jeanne stood for a minute, watching as Dr. Legear tended to Nicolas. Then with a furtive smile she went to meet her guest.

"Monsieur Bassenge?"

A gangly man with a pockmarked face was waiting by the window. He started as Nicolas's shouts echoed from the adjoining room, but Jeanne only shrugged. "One of the menials is having a tooth drawn," she said dismissively.

Bassenge shuddered. "Ah. That is never a pleasant procedure."

"Please, Monsieur—sit."

Jeanne showed him to a chair and crossed to where a silver tray held a decanter of port and several delicate silver-chased glasses. Monsieur Bassenge settled himself gratefully, and said, "I regret that my partner, Monsieur Bohmer, could not join me. He has taken to his sickbed over the very matter of which I desire to speak."

Jeanne offered him the silver tray. Bassenge nodded thanks and poured himself a glass. "I pray his discomfort is not serious," said Jeanne.

Bassenge shook his head mournfully. "This burden has leached the very will to live from a formerly robust man."

"If it is within my power to improve the situation," Jeanne said comfortingly, "you may of course count on me."

Bassenge finished his port. "Countess. It has come to my attention that you have influence with Antoinette."

"On certain issues." Jeanne poured herself a port and sipped it.

"Then I would like to make you aware of a rather lucrative proposition."

Jeanne turned and smiled at him, one of those radiant sunlit smiles that promised nothing but good fortune to the beholder. "Why then, Monsieur Bassenge, you have my *devoted* attention."

➤*I ATTEST NOW THAT GREED HAD NO PLACE IN MY thoughts that night. What shimmered before me was a means by which I could hasten my plans to regain the Valois' rightful estate. Because the instant that first burst of spectral light touched upon my eye, a design began to form . . .*

➤IT WAS LONG AFTER MIDNIGHT WHEN Jeanne and Retaux visited Monsieur Bohmer's workshop. Their way was lit by candelabras that cast flickering motes of gold and black across the room around them. In a corner Monsieur Bohmer sat in an armchair, still in his nightshirt and wincing with discomfort.

"I am not well," he gasped. "Not well at all."

And so it was left to Monsieur Bassenge to do the honors with the *rivière* necklace. He removed the red leather case from its cabinet and very slowly opened the lid, revealing what was inside to the astonished eyes of Jeanne and Retaux.

"All we ask is that you—*reintroduce* the idea of the necklace to Antoinette," Bohmer croaked.

"If a bargain were struck," Bassenge broke in quickly, "why then we could assure you of a generous commission."

"A *very* generous commission." Bohmer's rheumy eyes fixed beseechingly on Jeanne. "Please, Countess—won't you help us? With what we paid for these diamonds—why, the interest alone is ruining us."

Jeanne and Retaux exchanged a look; then the Comtesse's gaze was riveted once more on the supernaturally brilliant stones.

⇜ IT WAS NEAR DAWN BEFORE THE TWO OF them returned to Jeanne's rooms. Jeanne carefully shut and latched the door to her bedchamber, motioning for Retaux to keep his voice low so as not to wake Nicolas. Retaux sank onto a chaise beside a spinet arranged with Jeanne's latest passion: a collection of porcelain angels, painted and gilded like so many celestial baubles. He stared at them, then at Jeanne, who laughed and joined him beside the spinet.

"It was fantastic, wasn't it?" she said in a low voice.

"I've never seen its equal. That necklace could vastly improve a person's situation in life." He stood for a moment, musing, then added, "Of course the jewelers wouldn't just hand over the piece. They'd want an enormous advancement, or a guarantee . . ."

Jeanne gave him a sly smile. "Are we not already blessed with a benefactor possessing more than adequate means?"

"Rohan?" Retaux looked at her sharply. "No, Jeanne. That is a very dangerous idea."

She took a step away from him, to stand thoughtfully beside the spinet, studying the angels there as though they were chesspieces laid out on a board.

"A charming fellow," she said, moving until she stood facing him from across the spinet, "someone who is not as shallow as he'd like to have you think, once told me something worthwhile."

She fixed him with a teasing look. "The way to get what you desire . . ."

" . . . is to first know what everyone else desires."

He leaned forward on his elbows, giving her his full attention. Lips pursed, Jeanne gazed at the angels; then picked up two of them—one frail and thin, the other a robust cupid—and moved them apart from the rest.

"As we know," she said, "the jewelers have laid their hopes on Antoinette, to relieve them of their glimmering burden."

She looked up, her eyes locking with Retaux's. His lips parted but he said nothing, as Jeanne toyed with a tall, stern-faced angel.

"Then there is our benefactor—Rohan the devout." She placed the stoic angel in the center of the spinet. "He desires the one thing his wealth can't acquire: the position of Prime Minister. But what the Cardinal doesn't know—"

She picked up a graceful angel with the calm features of a Greek goddess. "—is that Antoinette herself secretly desires the necklace! But there are obstacles in her way . . ."

She moved the two angels, stoic and goddess, until they stood beside each other, then touched each one of them in turn. "Yet if Rohan could somehow make the transaction possible, the jewelers would find a home for their necklace—with Antoinette. And in gratitude for Rohan's help, Her Majesty would grant him the Prime Ministership."

Dreamily she leaned across the spinet, gazing at the angels as though entranced. Retaux stared at her intently, but when their eyes met he shook his head.

"There is one slight flaw," he said. "The Queen does not desire the necklace. She turned the jewelers down unequivocally."

Jeanne looked back at him. "You must keep abreast with current events, my love." She turned and stepped to her writing table, picked up a quill pen, and slowly drew its plume through her fingers. "It would seem that Antoinette has had a change of heart. As a matter of fact, I wouldn't be at all surprised if she were to write a letter expressing that very fact."

Retaux followed her. He stopped, plucked the quill from her hand, and thoughtfully stroked his cheek with it.

"Madame," he said at last, his eyes glowing at the thought of intrigue. "I thoroughly expected you to lead me to ruin at some point—but must it be in such a mad fashion?"

"Of course, my love." Her eyes were brilliant as Bohmer's diamond *rivière*. She leaned forward and touched her finger to Retaux's chin, a flush creeping across her bare arms and shoulders. "And that is for one reason only —

"Because it would make everything right."

A letter arrived at the House of Rohan the next day. The Cardinal was in his gardens, oblivious of the sun dancing on the ornamental lake where swans circled dreamily, and where the Comtesse de La Motte stood, shading her ivory skin with a parasol. A few yards away from her, Rohan sat at a breakfast table with Comte Cagliostro, the Cardinal reading his letter, the Comte absently peeling peaches with a jeweled dagger.

"I don't understand." Rohan frowned and held the gilt-edged stationery carefully between his fingertips, as though it might scorch him. "It makes no sense at all."

A servant appeared, bearing a cup of hot tea.

Rohan glanced at the steam wreathing the fine porcelain cup and scowled; his servant hastily blew on it, trying to cool it so that His Eminence might drink. With an impatient gesture Rohan waved the man away and sipped the tea, grimacing.

"Why does Antoinette wish to obtain this brutish trinket in such secrecy?" he asked, his voice troubled.

Jeanne bent to toss a scrap of bread at the feeding swans. "These are sensitive times," she said lightly. "Such an extravagance could cause further unrest among the people."

"Then why ensnare His Eminence in such a venture?" Cagliostro let a curl of peach fuzz fall to the ground. With a lascivious smile he devoured the rest of the moist fruit, spitting the pit in Jeanne's direction. She glared at him, turned to Rohan, and explained, "Antoinette seeks a discreet intermediary. Someone who could provide a firm guarantee to the jewelers should she be forced, by unforeseen circumstances, to default on her payment."

Two other figures approached the table. The first was Rohan's secretary, Abel Duphot.

"Uh hem." He cleared his throat, standing at attention. "I beg your pardon, Your Eminence . . ."

From behind Duphot stepped a pert young woman with pale blue eyes and an elfin smile. "But Mademoiselle Subur has arrived for her—"

He hesitated, taking in Jeanne and Cagliostro. "—her religious tutorial."

The Marquis Boullainvillers (Jeremy Clyde) and his wife (Wanda Ventham) take in the young orphaned Jeanne Valois (Hayden Panettiere).

Now twenty-four years old and a comtesse, Jeanne de La Motte-Valois (Hilary Swank) maneuvers through society to approach the woman she believes can help her reclaim her birthright: Marie Antoinette.

The luminescent Marie Antoinette (Joely Richardson) receiv[es] courtiers' applause for her performance . . .

. . . but Retaux de Vilette (Simon Baker) only has eyes for t[he] intriguing comtesse in the red dress.

An expert at social politics, Retaux begins to teach Jeanne the intricacies of court life, and how she can use such knowledge to obtain what she desires most.

Antoinette is offered the opulent necklace that will lead to her downfall.

The decadent Cardinal Rohan's (Jonathan Pryce) longing for Antoinette's favor makes him an excellent pawn in Jeanne and Retaux's plot.

Comte de Cagliostro (Christopher Walken) serves as counselor to Rohan, who looks to the man's mystic powers for guidance.

Jeanne's wayward husband, Nicolas de La Motte (Adrien Brody), returns, seeking a share of Jeanne's newfound wealth and a chance to rekindle their love.

In the Grove of Venus, Rohan meets "Antoinette" . . .

. . . as Jeanne and Nicolas anxiously watch their scheme unfold.

Back in possession of her childhood home, Jeanne uncovers the Valois crest and reclaims her family's lost honor at last.

Once her elaborate plot is discovered, Jeanne finds herself arrested and confined to the Bastille.

The tortured, broken Retaux receives his sentence of banishment from France.

Antoinette hears of Rohan's acquittal and realizes with anguish the dire consequences such a verdict holds for her and the monarchy.

Jeanne struggles as she is brought to be branded with a *V* for *voleuse* (thief).

After her escape from prison, Jeanne moves to London and shares her incredible story, never to return to France.

Mademoiselle Subur gave the Cardinal a sly sideways glance. Rohan only nodded brusquely and said, "Have her escorted to the private chapel. I will follow momentarily."

Duphot nodded. He turned and gestured for a servant to take the mademoiselle to a small chapel tucked beneath the trees in a corner of the garden. Jeanne took this slight distraction as an opportunity to speak.

"Your Eminence—you have improved your position with the Queen. Help her acquire this necklace, and the path to the Prime Minister's post will be a short one."

"I have grown extremely tired of treading that path on my hands and knees!" the Cardinal exploded. He looked at Cagliostro. "What have *you* to say?"

Cagliostro casually twirled his dagger, sunlight sparking from its jeweled pommel. "Though it galls me to agree with this woman, I do sense a resolution," he said in his smooth voice. "Stay the course."

Rohan paced a short distance away, holding the letter in his hand. At last he turned on them, fiercely.

"*No.*" He strode back to where Jeanne stood beside the table and slapped the letter down in front of her. "I have denounced my own character in writing. I have paid you exorbitant amounts to exert your influence. Yet my only request has been ignored! I want a private audience with Antoinette!"

Jeanne took a wary step backward, away from the raging Cardinal. "I mean no disrespect, but your reputation makes that impossible at this time." She looked pointedly to where Mademoiselle Subur flounced in front of the entrance to the private chapel.

"*I* make the terms now," Rohan countered icily. "Unless I meet with Her Majesty face to face, our arrangement is through." He fingered his golden crucifix, attempting to calm himself. "Now—if you will excuse me. An eager mind awaits."

He spun on his heel and headed toward the chapel. A quick look passed between Jeanne and Cagliostro. As Abel Duphot watched, they turned their backs to one another, and silence descended upon the Cardinal's gardens.

Chapter

NINETEEN

❧ ❦

It was afternoon before Jeanne and Retaux finally left the charmed circle of her bedchamber. They walked side by side through the narrow city streets, now and then exchanging a complicit lovers' smile that would have fooled no one: this was, after all, Paris. As they neared the marketplace their surroundings grew more oppressive—entire families living on the street, children playing in filthy open sewers while their mothers washed clothing a few feet away. The dirty walls were covered with scrawled imprecations against the monarchy, enlivened here and there by crude depictions of the Queen in lascivious poses. Jeanne stared at these thoughtfully as they passed, and Retaux shook his head.

"Jeanne. We must speak of this. Your plan—it was a fanciful idea, but the Cardinal's demand to meet the Queen has put it all beyond our reach."

Jeanne stopped to press a few coins into the hand of a small girl holding an infant. "I still believe there is a way," she said, and began walking once more.

"Jeanne, it can't be done."

She turned, placing her hand on his arm. "This is an opportunity that will never come again."

She gazed into his eyes, as though there were no crowd around them; as though they were back in her chambers with the candlelight dying and her porcelain angels throwing small shadows across the wall. "With the necklace, I will finally have a chance to get back what was taken from me. And that is all I ever wanted."

Retaux stroked her cheek tenderly. "If I could get it back for you, Jeanne, I would. But honestly, my Countess—I can't see the way."

She smiled then, drawing back a little from him before taking his arm. From the near distance the sound of a fiddle began to echo merrily through the afternoon. "Then I will show you the way," she said, leading him toward the music.

They rounded a corner and there was a traveling theatrical troupe, its makeshift stage set up beneath a billowing bright canvas tent, banners flapping wildly in the wind. A luridly painted poster had been pasted onto the wall alongside the stage.

QUEEN OF TARTS, OUR ANTOINETTE, it read. A few feet away a beautiful young woman, heavily made up and powdered, her arch features bearing a striking resemblance to those of the Queen of France. "Oh, Monsieur!" she squealed as an admiring gentleman leaned forward to whisper a suggestion in her ear.

Retaux gave the actress a sharp look, then looked at Jeanne. "If the Cardinal wishes to meet the Queen," she said, tipping her head toward the lissome corybante, "why then, he should meet the Queen!"

And she made a mocking curtsey toward the actress, who dimpled and gathered her own skirts, bowing graciously. Head held high, Jeanne once more took Retaux's arm, turned and steered him back to the marketplace.

"I am beginning to understand," he said, and added, "God help me! But Jeanne—even if by some miracle we *should* obtain the necklace, have you considered what will happen when no payment is made by Antoinette?"

Jeanne gazed at him unperturbed. "I should imagine that the stormy eye of Rohan will turn our way."

"Yes! And shit will rain upon us in biblical amounts. I for one do not desire to be its catch basin."

"Nor do I, thank you!" said Jeanne, laughing. "But listen to me—the good Cardinal will be furious, yes. But to implicate us would expose his own part in the scandal."

"And reveal that a mighty Rohan had been manipulated." Retaux shook his head admiringly. "You are right. His vanity could not bear the insult."

"And because of that, don't you think he will pay off the jewelers to cover up the affair?"

Retaux looked at her dubiously. "Perhaps—and then have both our throats cut in some dark and disagreeable place."

"I have thought of that and taken precautions." Jeanne picked up a bracelet of glittering green glass and examined it, turning it this way and that in the dying sunlight. "I believe there is a way to—*persuade*—His Eminence, that forgiveness is his only recourse. He will not lay a hand on us."

"And what of the resurrected husband?" Retaux went on, a touch of anxiety creeping into his voice. "Nicolas would betray us without a thought."

Jeanne replaced the bracelet. She turned to Retaux, her eyes imploring.

"Not if he's one of us," she said. "As hypocritical as it sounds, Nicolas would lend legitimacy to the household."

"And what is it I lend?" Retaux countered.

Jeanne touched his arm reassuringly. "Nicolas is a fact that will not go away. We might as well make use of his presence."

Once more she looked down at the table of paste jewelry, and with an enigmatic smile picked up a tiny ivory-colored angel on a string of black beads. She gave the vendor a few coins and turned away, but Retaux stopped her. He took the trinket and draped it around her throat, leaning forward to kiss the nape of her neck as he fastened the clasp.

"I suspect Nicolas would like to take up where he left off," he said, no longer able to mask his jealousy.

Jeanne shook her head. "He put any chance of that to rest forever, with his last outing to Rambouillet. Trust me on the matter."

Chapter

TWENTY

<hr>

Late that night only a single candle illuminated the window of Jeanne's bedroom, as befitting a chamber where complicated and somewhat furtive plans were being laid.

"I knew something grand was afoot." Nicolas sat facing the window, occupying the most comfortable armchair and sipping from Jeanne's very best brandy. His new linen shirt—just purchased from the tailor, and with a kiss from his not unwilling daughter part of the deal—hung loose about his chest, revealing where the top of a linen bandage still covered his nether parts. "And to think that you and the old dowager chaser came up with this, all on your own!"

He gave a sharp raucous laugh as Jeanne came in from the adjoining dressing room, cinching the ties on her lace and cotton nightgown. Nicolas stared at her longingly, but Jeanne was all business.

"Are you prepared to make such a binding commitment?" she demanded.

Nicolas made a mock bow, wincing slightly. "You can rest assured that I will be an asset to this venture."

Jeanne gave him a dubious look. "You can best help by showing restraint, however difficult that may be for you," she added coldly. She climbed into her four-poster bed, took a silver-plated brush from her nightstand, and began to run it through her hair. "It will be important in the days to come that all seems utterly normal within this residence. *Our* residence."

Nicolas stood, a trifle unsteadily, and balanced himself by grasping one of her bedposts. "'*Our* residence.' I like that part very much. But then what role does the gigolo play? Will he be an out-of-town cousin, visiting his cherished young *cousine*?"

Jeanne glared at him. "Retaux will do his part. You need only concentrate on *not* being yourself."

Nicolas swung around the bedpost, until he had brought himself beside her. "Don't be angry with me, Jeanne," he said softly. "I cannot help it: I am the way I am."

"And water seeks its own level, and pigs lie down in mud," she sniffed. Unperturbed, Nicolas reached to slide the brush from her hand, settled himself on the edge of the bed, and began to gently stroke her dark tresses. With every stroke, his air of bravado seemed to slip away.

"I thought of you often while we were apart." He stared with soft eyes at the nape of her neck. "Do you remember when I was stationed in Bremen, at the garrison on the Rhine? I would ride in field exercises all day long, with nothing on my mind but the thought of returning to my new bride. I could not wait to return each night, to that miserable garret where we lived—there to find your scented body lying upon the bed like a cut flower. I lived for it."

"As did I," said Jeanne sadly. "It is a shame that such devotion lacked stamina."

Nicolas shook his head. "You know as well as I that our marriage has always been an arrangement." He placed the brush on the nightstand and lay down alongside Jeanne. "You needed a title to gain access to the royal court. You took me on because I bought you that title."

He began to stroke her face, gently, lingering over the curves of her cheek, the soft line of her jaw and chin. "And in your eyes, I have never been more than a stepping stone," he ended wistfully.

Beneath his touch Jeanne felt herself stir. She stared at him, seeing for a moment the two of them as they had been then, so long ago, in a room far smaller than the one surrounding them, and darker; but far far warmer than this room was. "I saw something worthy in you at one time—even gallant. I wanted nothing more than to make a real marriage . . ."

He brought his face closer to hers then, his mouth finding hers and kissing her, so lightly she might almost have imagined it. When she did not move, he laid a tentative hand upon her shoulder, then slowly pulled the nightgown aside, revealing the white, softly gleaming skin beneath. He kissed her shoulder, his dark eyes finding her.

"Perhaps we could have that now?" he whispered.

He kissed her again, more forcefully this time, and felt her yield beneath him, returning his passion with her own. But even as his arms reached for her she raised a hand. She kissed her fingers, one-two-three-four; then touched them to his cheek.

"Ah, but Nicolas—you see, now it *is* an arrangement."

She rolled on her side, facing away from him; and with one quick cold breath blew out the candle. For a moment he remained on the bed; then without a sound stood and returned to his seat by the window, his brandy, the darkness all around them, and his memories.

Chapter

TWENTY-ONE

❧

It was a week before Jeanne's plan was to see the light of day—or rather, the pale gray and lavender of twilight in the gardens at Versailles. A heavy mist was gathering above the ornamental pools and lakes; the guards' lanterns shone eerily through the haze, like foxfire haunting the walls of the palace itself. Overhead a skein of swallows suddenly flashed against the darkening sky, startling one of the guards. He turned quickly, raising his lamp, but in looking at the sky he missed the two shadows crouching against an espaliered pear tree in the alcove behind him. A minute passed, and he continued on his rounds, leaving Jeanne and Cardinal Rohan to catch their breath and finally creep from the alcove out onto the palace lawn.

"This is a bit more intrigue than I bargained for," the Cardinal said hoarsely, running a hand across his brow. He followed her across the lawn, to where an allée of willow trees formed a twisting corridor that led to the Grove of Venus. Here, within a circle planted underfoot with sweet-smelling clover and chamomile, an alabaster statue of Venus rose from the center of a fountain spilling rosewater into a marble basin. Lilac trees surrounded the clearing, protecting them from prying eyes.

"You are to wait here," Jeanne whispered.

The Cardinal fussed with the lappets of his frock coat and looked around with excited anticipation. "I must confess, I am nervous."

Jeanne looked at him, surprised. "Give Her Majesty time to gaze upon you," she said, trying to sound both commanding and reassuring. "If she feels the moment is right, she will signal."

Jeanne demonstrated by inclining her head very slightly, and the Cardinal nodded. "I understand."

"And be ready to flee at a moment's notice."

He stared after her anxiously as she left him alone with only the statue for company.

She found Retaux and Nicolas where she had left them, hiding behind the cover of a neatly-trimmed hedge.

"We have the gardens to ourselves," said Nicolas, indicating the acres of greenery around them. Nicolas slid a flask from his pocket and sipped from it greedily.

"Is that necessary?" hissed Jeanne with an angry look.

"Yes, it is." Nicolas glared and took another swig. "The wound on my ass is barking like a bitch hound. I should be home convalescing."

"If you're to be a part of this, Nicolas," snapped Retaux, "then be a part of it."

Nicolas laid his hand on the hilt of his sword and glowered. "Do you doubt my enthusiasm for the undertaking?"

"Not at all, though your character in general seems ripe for discussion."

"You—" Nicolas started to draw his sword, but Jeanne stopped him.

"Monsieurs, this is not the time for a stag fight. Retaux, if you please, keep watch further down the path—"

Retaux shot Nicolas a furious look, but moved reluctantly down the path. Jeanne took a step forward, then tugged at a branch and motioned a figure to step from the greenery and join her. A woman in an alluring powder-blue dress stepped from the hedge. From the front of her stylish hat frothed a veil of silver tissue, not so much hiding as accentuating her arch features.

In the soft twilight, she resembled no one so much as Her Majesty the Queen.

"Say only what we have rehearsed, nothing more," commanded Jeanne in a low voice. "And have confidence."

The beautiful woman in blue tilted her head. "It is only acting, yes?"

"Yes," said Jeanne, "but it must be convincing."

"If he is a man," retorted the actress with a saucy smile in Nicolas's direction, "then I will convince him."

She turned and stepped carefully back through the hedge. Nicolas, gloating, sidled alongside Jeanne to a small gap in the hedge that afforded an unobstructed view of the Grove of Venus. Through it they could see Cardinal Rohan, pacing anxiously and rubbing his hands together in anticipation.

It had seemed hours to Rohan, but in fact only minutes passed before there was a slight rustle at the far end of the grove. He started, then turned, the breath catching in his throat.

From the moonlit trees stepped a ghostly figure in a flowing dress, itself the pale shimmering blue of moonlight. A sheer veil covered her face; in her slender fingers she clasped a blood-red rose. She walked into the center of the grove and stopped, staring at Rohan. He stared back, his mouth dry, unable for once to speak, or act; to do anything but gaze longingly upon her beauty. At last she gave him a single nod—the signal the Countess de La Motte had spoken of—and with a sigh of relief the Cardinal walked toward her.

A small wind lifted the veil from her face, giving him a momentary glimpse of her white skin and shining eyes, the smooth curve of her mouth. When he stopped before her she extended her hand, offering him the rose, and whispered, "Forgiveness is a rose with fragrance sweet."

He took the blossom, but his gaze never moved from her face. With a soft cry he suddenly dropped to his knee, gathering the hem of her dress to him and kissing it.

"If I have offended you, Your Majesty, I have suffered for it."

The woman in blue looked down, startled, her amazement mirrored in the faces of Jeanne and Nicolas where they watched in hiding.

"This—this is not necessary—" the woman in blue stammered.

"I remember the day you arrived at Versailles." Rohan's words came out in a rush. "A girl of fourteen with rosebud lips. I was a young bishop then, and well-liked . . . you trembled as I lay my hand upon your shoulder to offer the prayer of greeting. I—I felt there was a connection between that girl and that young man. A connection that transcended mere curiosity . . ."

The woman in blue stared down at him, her eyes soft. Unexpectedly, she reached down to caress his cheek.

"Forgiveness," she murmured tenderly.

From behind the hedge Jeanne and Nicolas watched, their astonishment undiminished; then stood up quickly as a warning voice hissed at them.

"Someone is coming!"

Retaux came bounding down the trail, looking anxiously over his shoulder. "Madame Campan and the Captain of the Guard," he gasped, pointing. "They have an assignation—quick!"

Just outside the far entrance to the grove, someone swept aside a willow branch. An instant later Antoinette's lady-in-waiting appeared, followed by Baron Courchamps, the Captain of the Guard. She fell to the ground, laughing, and the Baron fell on top of her, grinding his hips against hers and growling.

"Release the monster!" he said, moving her hand toward his groin. "It longs to prowl!"

With a squeal Madame Campan squirmed out from under him. "Release it yourself! I should like to see *that*!"

Giggling she ran toward the Grove of Venus; but before she could enter Jeanne had rushed through the hedge. "We must go, Your Eminence!" she cried. *"Now!"*

Rohan stumbled to his feet, staring mutely up at the woman in blue. Jeanne tugged at him, but he did not move, torn by his desire for the vision before him. His mouth opened to say farewell—but she was already gone, slipping through a break in the hedges and disappearing into the shadows.

"Your Eminence!" Jeanne said desperately. "Another second and I will leave you here to explain yourself—"

She grabbed his hand and hurried him from the grove. Behind them, where moments before the Cardinal had knelt, Madame Campan came running in a halfhearted effort to escape the Captain of the Guard. He grasped her about the waist, pulling her to him as he kissed her neck.

"Don't mark me!" she gasped. "My husband may be a fool but he is not blind."

The Baron Courchamps obediently drew back. As he did so, he caught a glimpse of a fleeting figure in pale blue hastening across the path.

"What was that?" he cried. He pushed aside Madame Campan and drew his sword. "Guards! Guards of the Palace!"

Madame Campan crouched in the shadow of the hedge, panicked. "I was never here, do you understand?" she cried hoarsely. "Never—"

She turned and scurried back to the palace. Still shouting for help, Courchamps forced his way through the hedgerow in pursuit of the intruder. Mere yards away and hidden by a turn in the path, the woman in blue stood in confusion, when suddenly a hand shot from the hedge and grabbed her.

"No!" she cried; then turned to see Retaux, motioning for her to be silent.

"Follow me," he mouthed, dragging her after him. They had only gone a little way when Nicolas came crashing after them.

"This way!" he gasped, pointing to yet another winding passage. Behind them they could hear the shouts of the palace guard as they arrived in the Grove of Venus. Nicolas shook his head in dismay, then took the woman's hand.

"I say we separate," he said, and dragged her after him.

"Nicolas!" cried Retaux. "Wait, damn you!"

"You there!" From behind Retaux came a bellowed command, as Courchamps and the palace guard emerged from the hedgerow. "Stand fast where you are!"

Retaux flashed them a despairing look, then sprinted after Nicolas. With a shout Courchamps and his guards gave chase.

The gardens of Versailles were bordered on one side by thick forest and marshland; on the other side by the King's Road. It was to the latter that Retaux thought he was heading, but after a quarter hour of running through brush and scrub he found himself at the reed-grown edge of the swamp.

"Damn!" He cursed under his breath, then looked back to see the thicket moving where the guards were beating their way through the brush. There was no other choice: he must hide in the swamp. Still cursing, he waded out into the mire; then took a deep breath and sank down beneath the surface of the muddy water.

A minute later Courchamps and his men reached the shore. They raced back and forth, seeking fruitlessly for footsteps in the spongy ground.

"He must have gone back toward the palace," Courchamps conceded at last. "That way—"

He turned and led the guards off in the opposite direction. From where he hid beneath an overhanging willow, the drenched Retaux watched, then turned and began to make his way toward the road.

It took him another quarter-hour, but finally he saw the appointed meeting place where a carriage waited. Retaux stumbled from the woods, dripping and covered with swamp-wrack, just in time to see Nicolas and the lady in blue come darting from across the road. At the carriage they halted while Nicolas assisted her inside. Two tiny poodles yipped and leaped into her arms, and Retaux watched as Nicolas swung himself in after her, shouting at the driver.

"Stop for nothing!"

The driver cracked his whip, as Retaux staggered toward them with a cry.

"Wait! Nicolas, wait—"

The carriage hurtled by. The last thing Retaux saw was Nicolas's face pressed to the window, one finger waved in a snide farewell as they racketed away from Versailles.

"Well," Nicolas said as Retaux's soaking figure

was lost to sight. "Now perhaps we will attend to more important matters . . ."

He turned to the woman across from him, the two little dogs on her lap. She stared back at him, smiling expectantly as he leaned forward and placed a hand upon her breast. Her shoulders arched, and she placed her own hand over Nicolas's. "Yes," she whispered.

As though given a command, the two poodles crept from her lap and retired to a corner of the rocking carriage. Nicolas eased himself onto the seat beside the woman, and tore the veil from her face. Feverishly he ran his hands across her shoulders as she pulled down her bodice to expose her breasts. Nicolas lowered his head to her nipple and teased it between his lips, as the woman moaned.

"Your Majesty," he murmured, and slid his hands beneath her gown.

❧ ❦

I n another, far more elegant carriage, Jeanne de
La Motte sat uneasily beside the Cardinal, giving him anxious looks as he stared balefully out the
window. He had not spoken a word since they left
Versailles. She sighed, glancing down, then drew
her breath in sharply: the Cardinal's hand was crimson, streaked with blood where his fist was
clenched around the rose given him by the woman
in blue.

"You have attempted to deceive me, Countess,"
he said in a hoarse whisper.

Jeanne swallowed, warily choosing her words.
"Deceive you, Your Eminence? It is not within my
character."

The Cardinal bared his teeth in a smile. "Do not make pretense with me, Countess." She shrank away as he leaned toward her, his breath hot on her face. "Antoinette is secretly in love with me. Deny it if you will, but do not ask me to play the fool."

Jeanne dipped her head, struggling to keep relief from shading her voice. "How could she hope to hide it from Your Eminence's most canny reception?" she said. "Perhaps—perhaps a letter from you, stating your true feelings, would be in order . . ."

The Cardinal brought the rose to his face and breathed in deeply; then looked at Jeanne and smiled.

"Yes," he said thoughtfully. He brushed the rose across his lips. "Yes, I think perhaps it might be."

⤛ AND SO THE BARGAIN WAS STRUCK. MONsieurs Bohmer and Bassenge, jewelers to Her Majesty the Queen, were at last to have a buyer for their precious *rivière:* none other than the Cardinal himself, acting as intermediary for the Queen. The Cardinal was to place the necklace in Antoinette's hands by way of Her Majesty's trusted confidante, the Countess de La Motte-Valois. Rohan was informed—again, by the good graces of the Countess—that Her Majesty would pay for the necklace in full in three months time, on the day of the Feast of the Assumption.

And Cardinal Rohan himself stood as guarantor for the full price of the Queen's necklace, should any misfortune befall it—

A fact which began to weigh increasingly heavily upon the Cardinal's mind.

➤ THE SCRYING WAS ARRANGED FOR MIDNIGHT. That was the hour determined by Cagliostro. Rohan, more superstitious, was secretly unnerved by the time, and the setting—the catacombs of the House of Rohan, a place the Cardinal did not care to set foot under the most benign of circumstances. Still, once all had been determined, he made certain that he was there a good quarter-of-an hour early, to light the heavy beeswax tapers himself, and see to it that no earthly intruders disturbed the catacomb.

The chamber was huge, hewn out of the sandstone beneath the ancient château. The tombs of Rohan's ancestors rose in somber splendor all around; an empty space in the center of the room awaited more recent additions. It was here that Cagliostro stood, sword in hand, his flowing velvet robes falling in dark pools about his booted feet. On a marble table at his side lay the red leather case that held the diamond *rivière*. Candles surrounded it, and a handful of dried herbs scattered there by the Comte. Rohan sat across from the table in a high-backed chair, his face pale and watchful. Cagliostro looked at him, inclining his head, then raised his sword with one hand and with the other drew back the folds of his robe.

"Behold a Dove!" he cried. "A child born under a gifted star."

Pressed against the Comte's legs was a child: a girl of no more than nine years, with corpse-white skin and enormous, melancholy eyes the color of night. She was barefoot, clad only in a long white chemise with a yellow sun embroidered upon the breast. Cagliostro gazed down at her, then took a step backwards, leaving her alone in the center of the room. From a pocket in his robe he withdrew a carafe of clear liquid. He crossed to the table and placed the carafe atop the red leather case, then lifted his sword and made three passes over it, chanting softly.

"When a Dove gazes into sanctified water, she can see with great clarity into the future."

As though sleepwalking, the child stepped toward Rohan. She stopped in front of him, took his slender hand in her tiny one, and placed it against her cheek, all the while staring fixedly into his face. The Cardinal stared back, entranced by the girl's piercing eyes. Cagliostro lifted his sword a final time, then bowed and laid it across the back of the table. He turned and crossed to the girl, and gently turned her until she faced the carafe of water.

"Tell us what you see, child," he commanded.

As though a breeze stirred them the candle flames leaped and guttered. Atop the leather case, the carafe of crystal water shivered. The Dove stared at it, her eyes huge; then made a small sound as her face grew contorted.

"It—it is horrible." Her voice was unnaturally high and strained, as though it hurt her to speak. "I see a rotting corpse in Roman purple vestments. Worms—worms eat through its eyes!"

Rohan whirled to Cagliostro. "What is this?" he hissed.

Cagliostro only looked at the child and shook his head. "You have gone too far ahead of us," he said gravely. "We seek answers in the near future. Concentrate, my Dove."

The child nodded, focusing once more upon the carafe. Again the candle flames jumped and sputtered; again the carafe trembled.

"I see a beautiful lady," the girl whispered at last. "She is the object of much attention."

She shut her eyes, struggling to maintain her focus; then opened them again. "It is . . . the Queen."

Cardinal Rohan sucked his breath in, staring at her raptly.

"I see the Cardinal," the child went on with great

effort. "He kneels before her. She—she places an object around his neck."

Rohan's eyes narrowed, and he smiled: he could almost see her there before him, light streaming from her fingers as the Queen smiled back down at him. On the table before the Dove, the crystal carafe began to shake violently upon the leather case.

"It—it is round," the Dove stammered. "And made of—of—"

"Fight, child!" commanded Cagliostro. "Fight to push back the mist!"

"Gold!" The child's voice rose to a shriek. "It's made of gold!"

With a sound like a pistol report the carafe shattered. The Dove screamed and collapsed. "Dear God in heaven!" cried Rohan.

Quick as thought Cagliostro was on his knees beside her, scooping her up and carrying her to a tomb. He laid her on top of it, pulling a hand mirror from his robes and holding it before her face.

"It is taxing for one so young." He stared at the mirror, frowning, then sighed deeply as the glass fogged. "But she will recover."

The Cardinal crossed to a table covered with a damask cloth, laden with fruits and several bottles of wine. He filled a crystal goblet and drank from it, staring into the shadows of the chamber. After a moment Cagliostro stepped up behind him.

"Did her vision hold meaning for you?"

Rohan took another draft of wine. "The seal of

the Prime Minister takes the form of a medallion."
He paused, then added triumphantly, "A medallion
of pure gold."

Cagliostro plucked a grape from a silver bowl
and popped it into his mouth. "It is merely a preter-
natural apparition of what could occur," he said in a
warning tone. "It is not a certainty."

Rohan nodded uneasily. "I understand," he said
at last. "I too have doubts. But it is my belief that we
each possess the power to influence our own des-
tinies. And so I will do what is within my ability to
make this come to pass . . ."

"Whatever is necessary?" asked Cagliostro
softly.

The Cardinal nodded. "Whatever is necessary."

A short time later, Cagliostro walked briskly
through the square, making his way home from the
House of Rohan. As he approached an alleyway, a
figure stepped from the shadows.

It was Jeanne. "Did all go well?" she asked, a
hint of teasing in her voice.

Cagliostro shook his hair back and stared at her.
"I was brilliant," he said, holding her gaze. "Of
course."

They stood there, gazing at each other, a growing
complicity in their faces so that after a moment one
might have thought each reflected the other.

"You'll have no trouble with him now," said
Cagliostro with a tight smile. He continued on his
way.

Chapter

TWENTY-THREE

I t was not Rohan's custom, ever, to wait to do
what was necessary. The very next night found
him crossing the Place de Dauphine, heading for
the Hotel Belle Image. The Cardinal's secretary and
two of his guards accompanied him; but it was to
Abel Duphot that the Cardinal entrusted the red
leather case that held the diamond *rivière*. At the
door to the Hotel Belle Image they stopped. Rohan
turned to Duphot.

"I will take it now," he said, glancing around to
make sure they were not observed. "You are to wait
here with my guard, until I return or signal you."

Abel Duphot nodded, handing him the case. "Of

course, Your Eminence," he said, and bowed. "I will await you."

Rohan entered the hotel and climbed the narrow winding stairs with distaste, taking in the desultory wallpaper, the damp carpet underfoot and the faint scent of moldering upholstery that hung above everything. At the door to the Countess de La Motte's chambers he hesitated, then knocked.

"Your Eminence." Rosalie, the Countess's chambermaid, met him with lowered eyes. "This way, please."

Once inside, Rohan found a more elegant scene. The Countess and her husband sat playing backgammon near a glowing fire. There was a table set with fruits and cheese, a bottle of very good sauternes, the warm light of numerous beeswax candles.

"Your Eminence," said Jeanne, rising and curtseying. "Please, join us."

The Cardinal stepped quickly past her, glancing out the window to the street below. "You said we would have word tonight," he said, his voice clouded with anxiety. "You said—"

"It is early still." Jeanne settled back beside her husband. "And it is a good afternoon's ride from Versailles. Please, sit—"

The Cardinal sat, the leather case on his knees. Jeanne and Nicolas continued their game; Rosalie busied herself with pouring wine that the Cardinal did not touch. He continued to stare edgily at the window, and once or twice stood to pace impatiently back and forth across the room.

And then, at last, there came a knock at the door. Rohan sat up attentively, as Rosalie hurried to greet the newcomer. A minute later she reappeared, escorting a handsome man wearing a black cape over the gold livery of a royal messenger.

It was Retaux. He swept back his cape and bowed deeply to the Cardinal, then turned to Jeanne, being careful not to meet her eyes.

"My Lady Countess," he said, producing a leather pouch and taking a letter from it. Rohan watched Retaux avidly as she read.

"It is a dispatch from Antoinette," she said, and handed it to the Cardinal for inspection. "The item of interest is to be turned over to this man, her messenger, for delivery to the Queen."

Rohan read the note, then gave Retaux a piercing look. "Do you have confidence in this man?" he asked Jeanne sharply.

Jeanne nodded. "His name is Argille. He attends the Queen's chambers." She motioned at the red leather case in his lap. "May I?"

The Cardinal's hands tightened around the case. "I am responsible for this object, to the sum of over one million gold Louis," he said, his voice taut. "I repeat my question, Countess. Do you have confidence in this man? Speak carefully—"

His gaze grew dark and threatening. "You will be accountable, Countess."

Jeanne gave a small shrug. "Monsieur Argille is not without faults. He drinks, and does well with chambermaids."

Retaux glanced down, feigning embarrassment. Jeanne shot him a condescending look, and added, "Yet when it comes to his devotion to the woman he serves, no one can compare to Argille. His fidelity is such that if I were not so joyfully bound to the Count, I daresay that Argille would have my heart."

In his chair, Nicolas frowned; but Rohan did not notice. For another minute he stared at Retaux. Finally he handed the case to Jeanne. Without a word she handed it to Retaux, who bowed hastily and took his leave. After he had left, the Cardinal once more walked to the window and stared down uneasily.

"That man is familiar to me somehow."

Jeanne shook her head. "Perhaps you've seen him at the palace."

Nicolas stood and joined his wife. "The fellow had rather a common face, I thought."

Cardinal Rohan ignored them. He opened the door to the balcony and went outside, leaning over the railing to get a final look at Retaux. Jeanne and Nicolas glanced worriedly at each other.

"Your Eminence," Nicolas said quickly. He poured another glass of sauternes, stepped out onto the balcony, and thrust it at the Cardinal. "You will no doubt reap untold rewards from what you have done."

Rohan watched as Retaux exited the hotel and started toward the street, to where a hired coach waited. Abel Duphot and the two guards looked at him impassively.

"Wait!" the Cardinal shouted down to Duphot. "Detain that man—"

Abel Duphot stepped in front of Retaux as one of the guards grabbed his arm. Rohan whirled to confront Jeanne and Nicolas. "If he is a messenger of the royal house," he demanded, his voice like iron, "then why is he not in a carriage from the palace? Answer me that."

Jeanne and Nicolas exchanged a swift look. Jeanne clasped her hands together tightly: she had not considered this. Before she could utter a word, her husband stepped forward.

"The conveyance is plain for reasons of secrecy," he said smoothly. "It goes without saying, Her Majesty has taken every precaution not to draw attention to this exchange."

Rohan stood and mused on this for a long time. In the street below Retaux stood at attention, the red leather pouch still in his hands. At last Rohan turned and stared down from the balcony, giving a nod to Duphot. His secretary stepped aside, and Retaux pulled his arm indignantly from the guard. Holding his head high, he crossed to the waiting carriage and clambered inside. The Cardinal continued to stare uneasily as the carriage clattered off through the empty square.

Jeanne took her place beside him and laid a hand on his arm. "Your Eminence," she said in a low, reassuring voice. "Put aside any fears you may have. I give you my solemn oath that the necklace will find its proper place this very night."

The Cardinal did not take his eyes from the street. After a long time he turned, and left in silence.

Chapter

TWENTY-FOUR

◆

They were not greedy, not at first. During the two months that followed they sold only a small portion of the diamonds. Nicolas traveled to Amsterdam and performed most of the transactions there, so as not to attract attention. Once they had the money safe in hand, Jeanne needed to retreat to someplace far from Paris, where she could enjoy her newfound fortune in comfort, and anonymity.

For her, there was never any question as to where that place would be. It was one of the few times of pure happiness that she experienced in her life, riding in a cabriolet from Paris, three wagons accompanying them, filled with the new furnishings they had purchased—clothes, enough furniture for all three of them to live together in peace and prosperity.

Jeanne rode in the carriage with Retaux beside her. And when they mounted the last hill, and Jeanne had her first glimpse of the sprawling estate, she could scarce keep the tears from her eyes, or her heart from thudding within her breast.

"Hurry, Monsieur, hurry! Please," she added as an afterthought, as though she were a child again commanding her father, and not a grown woman giving orders to a carriage driver. Retaux laughed, and bounded up to join the driver, taking the reins from him.

"If the Countess wishes to make haste, why then we make haste!"

The cabriolet rolled down the hill, its wheels thundering. Jeanne looked up at Retaux, clutching her hat to keep it from blowing away, and she could see in his face how much joy it gave him, to see her thus: happy and fulfilled at last.

They reached the château at midday. The county barrister was there, one of those ruddy-faced countrymen who seem more at ease behind a plow horse than overseeing an exchange of property. But he had done his job well: the papers were in order, the interlopers who had displaced Jeanne from her home all those years before were now themselves displaced, hastily piling the last of their belongings into a wagon in the courtyard.

"The château is now in your ownership, Countess." The barrister smoothed down a few greasy strands from his ancient wig and handed her the documents. Jeanne took them, waiting for the old aristocrat and his family to haul themselves into their wagon, and stood cold-eyed as they drove off.

She felt no more remorse at that moment than they had when they witnessed her family tossed from their home decades before.

"Countess?" Retaux stood beside her and held out his arm. "May I escort you into your home?"

Inside all the rooms were empty; and yet for Jeanne they were full, noisy with remembered laughter and crowded with the revenants of all whom she had loved most, and lost. She went from room to room, her footsteps growing ever more quick upon the cold stone floor; quick and almost frenzied. She was looking for something, yet she almost could not recall what it was—

Until at last she stood within the main parlor. A cavernous room, empty as all the rest, save for an immense stone fireplace covered by a woven tapestry. She strode to the fireplace, her steps echoing through the vast space, grabbed the tapestry with both hands and yanked it from the mantel.

It pooled at her feet but Jeanne took no notice of it. Her eyes were upon the symbol carved into the wooden mantel: her family crest, surmounted by curving letters each a handspan high.

VALOIS

Her name. She sank to her knees and wept then, knowing she was home; home again, at last.

✒ A WEEK PASSED. IT WAS HIGH SUMMER, and each morning Jeanne awoke feeling as though it were her birthday: the joy not only of new discoveries to be made within the château, but of Retaux's face on the pillow beside her, the sounds of servants talking and calling and singing outside, the play of light upon the château's stone walls and on the water of the nearby lake.

One afternoon found her sitting on the bank of the stream that flowed there. She wore not damask and lace but a simple loose shift of linen and homespun, tied at the waist with blue ribbons. Her hair was unbound; at her feet was a basket of wildflowers, which she was tossing dreamily onto the brook's surface, watching them drift away into the golden light. At the edge of the stream stood Retaux, clad as Jeanne was in rustic glory—leather breeches, open linen blouson, a cane fishing pole in his hand. He'd seen no fish at all since arriving here hours ago, but one would never have guessed that from his expression: he looked happy, luxurious even, surrounded by nothing but sky and sun and breeze-blown grasses.

"Do you recall the look on Nicolas's face when we cut apart the necklace?"

At his words Jeanne looked over and smiled indulgently. Retaux flicked his line again, and added, "His nostrils flared as though his face were a giant bellows. He could embark on a spending spree that would be talked about for four generations."

Jeanne laughed, tossing another wildflower and smoothing her dress over her knees. "He's never been one for subtlety. We'll need to return to Paris, and see that he shows a little restraint."

From the narrow country road behind them came the lazy clop-clop of a dray horse. Jeanne turned to see the local priest, his rosy face smiling from beneath his broad-brimmed hat.

"I received the invitation to your gala tomorrow night, Countess." He waved a very large envelope, his smile broadening. "Just what our little village needs! A few high spirits!"

Jeanne waved back. The priest tipped his hat and rode on. Retaux stood, watching her silently, until she turned and saw him. The two of them gazed at each other for a long time without speaking. Then Retaux's fishing pole gave a twitch: he straightened, staring with great concentration at the water.

"I think I've got a nibble!"

Grinning, Jeanne playfully tossed a handful of flowers at him. "You'll catch a cold before you catch a fish."

"Woman, you question my prowess with a pole?" With a mock growl he leaped toward her, and Jeanne tried to dart behind a tree. He caught her there, pinning her against the trunk, the two of them laughing helplessly. But after a minute they grew quiet, and stood gazing tenderly at each other, Retaux's hand tracing the strong line of her cheek.

"I see you in a whole new light here," he said softly. "This place suits you."

Jeanne nodded. She reached to stroke the leaves on an overhanging branch, and said, "It is where I belong."

"I envy you." Retaux's voice broke slightly. He hesitated. "I cannot say that I have ever truly had that sensation. Not really . . ."

He looked away, but Jeanne gently took his face in her hands and turned it back to her. "This would not have been possible without you, Retaux. I know that. I want this place to be ours."

He stared at her yearningly—wanting to believe, yet not quite able to.

"We're not free and clear yet, my Countess. Have you forgotten? The Feast of the Assumption is in three days. When that day arrives and no payment has been made for the necklace, we'll have Rohan to face."

"We'll take precautions to protect ourselves."

She stood on tiptoe, kissing the arched curve of his neck. "I promise. But for now, let's just entertain the possibilities . . ." He gazed down, then embraced her. For this moment, at least, the possibilities seemed endless.

THE NEXT EVENING THE COURTYARD OF Jeanne's château was crowded with horses and carts and waiting servants, as all the neighboring countryside gathered to honor the new chatelaine. Inside Retaux stood, his face glowing as he held up a goblet and let his voice ring out through the sudden hush that fell across the ballroom.

"To the House of Valois, and the Countess who makes it shine!"

"To the Countess!"

"To the House of Valois!"

All those assembled toasted her, their voices and cheers echoing Retaux. Jeanne stood in the midst of the crowd, eyes brilliant; as the goblets were quaffed and lowered, the musicians broke into a reel, and a press of men gathered around, urging her to dance. Lowering her head demurely, she thanked them all, and reached for Retaux. He took her hand and the two of them led the reel, laughing as the rest joined in, dancing through the night.

Retaux's worst fears about Jeanne's husband were correct: once he returned to Paris, Nicolas de La Motte immediately became engaged in his favorite pastimes. He had summoned one of the city's more esteemed tailors to come to Jeanne's chambers—after all, one could not expect the Count de La Motte to walk about the city dressed as a common soldier! Now Nicolas lay on Jeanne's bed, on his side; his wound, while not serious, was still extremely uncomfortable. To ease the pain he was eating expensive chocolates from a silver box, and wearing a delectably soft quilted morning coat, lined with down-filled silk. On the table before him the tailor had spread the jacket and breeches of a custom-made suit for Nicolas to admire. The tailor's daughter had accompanied her father to the flat, and Nicolas found himself admiring her as well.

"Brocade, is it?" Nicolas asked, running his hand across the cloth.

"The finest."

"What else?" Nicolas craned his neck to peer into an overflowing trunk on the floor. "I want to see it all. Everything, everything, everything!"

The tailor snapped his fingers, and his daughter rushed to display more outfits. When she held up an embroidered waistcoat to him, Nicolas smiled and glanced at the tailor.

"Is this elegant vision your daughter?"

"Yes, Count. My eldest."

Nicolas leaned forward, locking eyes with her and extending his hand toward the chocolate box. "You are very lovely, my dear."

She smiled coquettishly. Nicolas plucked a chocolate from its container and licked it, slowly. "Have you ever considered a life in the theater?" he asked, then bit into the chocolate and with a practiced tongue extracted the creamy filling. The girl stared at him, her face reddening, and with a small gasp turned away, grabbing a chair to keep from falling. Nicolas grinned: no, he had not lost his touch.

"Madeline! What are you doing — *vites, vites —*"

As the tailor scolded his daughter, Nicolas with some effort pulled himself from the bed and walked stiffly to the window. Staring out at the street below, he sucked the last bit of cream from his chocolate and popped the shell into his mouth; then licked his fingers, oh so slowly, until every lingering mote of chocolate was gone. He stood there for some time, a pallid-faced figure in a sumptuous dressing gown, gazing into the midday with dark and soulless eyes.

A t the Chapelle de Versailles, King Louis XVI was also finding much to give him pleasure.

"The plasterer could not reach that high edifice," he explained proudly to House Minister Breteuil. "So, you see, I myself devised a system of pulleys by which he could be elevated."

Beaming, and for the fifth time that morning, the King demonstrated the pulleys to Breteuil. The House Minister blinked, trying to hide tears of boredom. "Fascinating, Your Majesty," he said. He coughed discreetly. "I must say—it is stunningly resourceful."

"Yes!" beamed the King. "This way, if you please,

Minister—I will see if we can get him to once more make the ascent—"

Breteuil stared over to where the hapless plasterer crouched in a corner, hoping to evade discovery. Breteuil gave him a warning gesture, and the laborer stumbled into a passage to seek refuge. Breteuil turned quickly back to the King.

"If you please, Your Majesty," the Minister announced; he had just sighted Antoinette a short distance away, walking in the garden with Madame Campan and her other ladies-in-waiting. "I forgot that I have some business to discuss with Her Majesty, regarding, er, some matters of import."

Louis was wandering with a vague expression, back toward the scaffold. "Yes, yes of course," she said absently. "Very good, Minister, thank you . . ."

Breteuil waited until the King's back was to him, then sighed with relief and started for Antoinette.

"And now, look who is approaching us," whispered Madame Campan. Antoinette glanced over from behind her fan, and saw not her House Minister but Monsieur Bohmer, the court jeweler. "Whatever can he want?"

Antoinette shook her head very slightly. "I cannot imagine," she murmured.

Monsieur Bohmer scuttled toward them, smiling brightly. He puffed up in front of Her Majesty, bowed until his wig threatened to part company with his head, then straightened. "Your Majesty," he gasped, redfaced, and extended a hand. "With the most esteemed compliments of Bohmer and Bassenge, court-appointed jewelers."

In his outstretched hand was the red leather jewelry case. Antoinette gazed down at it, nonplussed, but made no move to take it.

"If you please, Your Majesty. It is a bejeweled amulet. A token of our appreciation for your patronage these many years."

With a muted *snap* he opened the case to display an amulet, a teardrop-shaped sapphire on a heavy silver chain. It glistened in the sun like a fragment of sky that had fallen into the jeweler's hand. Antoinette hesitated, and tentatively took the jewelry box. With a broad smile, Bohmer bowed once more; then, spying the House Minister bustling toward them, he turned and hastily retreated.

"Your Majesty." Breteuil came up beside her, pausing to catch his breath. "I trust Monsieur was not disturbing you?"

"That jeweler has been grinning like a jackal all afternoon." She held up the jewelry box, removing a small note from it. "And now this—"

She unfolded the note and read, "'Madame, we are at the pinnacle of happiness with our recent arrangement with you. We take great satisfaction in knowing that the most beautiful creation in all the world will adorn the most exemplary of queens.'"

She lifted an eyebrow and turned questioningly to Breteuil. The House Minister looked concerned.

Frowning, he said, "I am not certain what to make of it."

Antoinette tapped the note against her pouting lower lip. "I think only one explanation can possibly suffice."

Breteuil and Madame Campan leaned closer to her with great interest, as Antoinette pronounced, "Monsieur Bohmer has gone quite mad."

Madame Campan bridled. "How embarrassing for his family!"

But House Minister Breteuil's expression grew more distressed. He turned to watch Monsieur Bohmer's portly figure receding into the shadows of the garden.

There is trouble in this, he thought, and remained thoughtfully at Her Majesty's side.

Chapter

TWENTY-SEVEN

❧

There were few pleasures that Nicolas de La
Motte had ever been able to resist: certainly
not women, nor fine clothes, nor the opportunity to
promenade upon the Rue de Amalie in late spring-
time, showing off the latter to the admiring eyes of
the former. The elite market arrondissement was
crowded with common people ogling wares they
could not afford, and aristocrats making their way
to the next round of fittings for fashionable new
clothes. And so it was an ideal spot not just for
Nicolas to display his grand new walking stick, but
for the gadfly Camille Desmoulins to continue de-
claring his private and very noisy war upon the
aristocracy.

"Look at them!" he shouted, spittle flying from his mouth as he flung his arm outward in Nicolas's direction. "Useless parasites, preying upon us—sucking our lifeblood, and our children's!"

The thoroughfare was packed with beggars and *putins*, servants going about their masters' work, women hawking bits of rags and the blackened heels of dried bread that were all that was available to the common folk in those famished days. Men were doing a brisk business selling scurrilous broadsheets attacking the royal family and their hangers-on. Nicolas paused to watch Desmoulins shove a handful of pamphlets at a young woman, who turned away quickly.

"If they could," Desmoulins cried, "those of the Palace Versailles would float above us in golden air balloons and with haughty glee piss upon us, and laugh at our vulgar existence. They expect us now to cheerfully fester in our own stink! To empty our own purses in order to pay for their debaucheries! When will we say, enough? When will we no longer be ruled like stupid, dull-eyed cows?"

He threw his spurned pamphlets into the air, raging, "What good is life, if one is unable to muster a single instant of joy from it? There must be reform! The King and his foreign harlot drain the life's blood of our national character with their easy ways! We must raise our voices in anger and drown out their moans of decadent pleasure! What was once only whispered must now be plainly spoken aloud: everyone wants to be rid of the damned Monarchy! To shed our shackles for something good, and new! Something born of the people — but new freedoms are not purchased with words alone. Only violence on a grand scale will bring about such change!"

From the watching throng a man called out drunkenly. "And as we march against pike and cannon, where will you be? Cheering us on from the nearest café table?" The crowd booed him roundly. Desmoulins took this as encouragement, and began imprecating them even louder. "Hardly, you dull oaf! I will be among you! And it is among those united ranks that I intend to die. And I shall be sorely put out if I do not linger long enough to dip my finger into my draining life's blood, and write upon the pavement where I have fallen, "France is free at last!"

His voice was drowned out by the crowd's cheers. A small group of roughnecks began pushing around the unfortunate drunk, who quickly staggered off to save himself. Nicolas watched, amused.

"I think it sad," said a voice beside him. He turned and saw the pretty young woman who had refused Desmoulins' incendiary pamphlets. She glanced at him, blushing, but went on, "When Antoinette first arrived from the Austrian court, they loved her — her youth and energy, the way she lured that oaf Louis from his shell and made a man of him. And now that times are bad, they call her a foreign bitch, and blame famines and floods and frosts on her. And because she will not or cannot change, they fear her openness and vitality. Her greatest flaw is that she cannot hide what she is."

Nicolas bowed to her. "You are as eloquent as you are elegant, Mademoiselle. Might I—"

But the girl was already gone. Nicolas shrugged, then went on his way.

He lifted his hat to several pretty young women, and gave a hearty greeting to the proprietor of a patisserie which Nicolas favored for its *chocolats* and *petit fours*. He did not, however, take notice of a jeweler who stood scowling on the other side of the street, watching Nicolas with an expression of severe disapproval.

And he did not—to his later regret—take notice of the gendarme the jeweler summoned, with many gesticulations and muttered oaths in Nicolas's direction. No: Nicolas was much too busy gaining the attention of another very young mademoiselle in sky-blue silk that set off her honey-colored curls, and a complexion so fresh it had seen neither pox nor powder in all its sixteen years. She was gazing transfixed at Desmoulins, clutching a parcel to her breast and literally trembling as she listened to his ravings.

"Quite a lot of excitement this morning, yes?" Nicolas sauntered up alongside her and flashed one of his most extravagant smiles.

"Ah, oui!" The girl turned to him with shining

eyes. "Desmoulins speaks with such fiery passions!"

Nicolas lowered his head. "Fiery passion happens to be the very attribute I hold most dear. . . ."

The mademoiselle's eyebrows lifted. Nicolas smiled and reached for her arm, but at that moment a hand descended upon his shoulder.

"Pardon me, Monsieur."

He turned to find himself staring into the broad suspicious face of a gendarme. Nicolas lifted his hands innocently. He gave a sideways wink at the girl, and said, "Ah—but I was not bothering the mademoiselle—"

The gendarme shook his head, cocking his thumb over his shoulder. "Monsieur, a few of the merchants here have informed me that you have been selling diamonds, without benefit of your own premises."

Nicolas gave a little laugh, relaxing on his walking stick. "They misunderstand—I am a licensed broker of precious stones. I trade frequently here and in Amsterdam."

The gendarme nodded. "I thought as much. So, Monsieur will not object to producing credentials to that effect."

Nicolas smiled and began to go through his pockets. At his side, the young mademoiselle made a quick curtsey to the gendarme and hurried off. Nicolas slapped his thigh, then drew his hand to his forehead, miming surprise. "Of course—how could I be so foolish! I have left them in my rooms at the hotel. If you'd care to accompany me there, we can clear up this matter in quick fashion."

The gendarme clicked his heels together. "I think we should, Monsieur."

They began to walk, the gendarme to Nicolas's right at the roadside. A few passersby regarded them curiously; Nicolas smiled and looked unperturbed. As they turned a corner an elderly woman pushing a cart full of flowers approached them, bunches of violets and lilies-of-the-valley and tea roses piled high on top of straw and croker sacks. Nicolas eyed the woman, pausing to doff his hat at her; then kicked aside the cart so that its contents went flying on top of the gendarme.

"Halt!" the man shouted, leaping across the strewn blossoms to grab at Nicolas's cape. But Nicolas was already gone: the cape fluttered uselessly in the man's hands, while the flower-seller wept and railed, beating at the hapless gendarme and screaming for help.

"Stop him! Stop that man!" The gendarme pushed aside the woman and gave chase. Nicolas darted into the street, narrowly avoiding being crushed by a hay wagon. The draft horses reared and whinnied, backing into another wagon and sending its load of potatoes rolling across the road. Nicolas took advantage of this diversion to double-back along the far side of the street, heading for a bridge.

"Damn!" He cursed and hesitated: there were two other gendarmes, chatting with the same pretty young girl he'd been conversing with moments before. Shouts and confused cries echoed up along the road; the gendarmes turned and saw Nicolas with one of their fellows in pursuit.

"Stop him! Stop—"

There was nothing to be done. Nicolas looked one way and then another: he was trapped. The young woman gave a shriek as the gendarmes lunged toward him. With a desperate oath Nicolas crossed himself, leaped onto the railing of the bridge, took a deep breath and dove into the Seine thirty feet below. His last thoughts were not of God, however, nor even of his beautiful wife, but of the diamonds he had secreted in his pocket, and how they would certainly be lost in the river.

Chapter

TWENTY-EIGHT

ᴥ❧❦ᴥ

S ainted Mother of Jesus, I nearly soiled myself!"
As her husband swore and shivered in his
hip bath, Jeanne walked over to the window and
stared out yet again, fearful of seeing the gendarmerie. Retaux stood beside her. As Nicolas
began once more to tell of his escape, Retaux gave
him a disgusted look and pulled the curtain aside.

"Good thinking to run straight back here," he
sneered. Behind him Nicolas pulled himself groan-
ing from the bath. He grabbed a robe and slid it on,
then reached for a glass of cognac with a trembling
hand. "That way they can have us all in one neat
bundle."

Nicolas drained his glass and shoved it aside. He

yanked a dagger from the table and in one fluid motion leaped to push Retaux against the wall, the dagger at his throat.

"Shut up, or I swear I'll cut that contemptible tongue right out of your head!"

Retaux stared at him defiantly. "You are a pompous fool, and an imbecile to boot. Go ahead and add *murderer* to that list, but be quick about it!"

Nicolas snarled, but as he pressed the dagger closer a hand clamped upon his shoulder.

"You've had a scare, and I know you are upset." Jeanne spoke soothingly, belying the strength of her grasp. "But you must maintain your temper! Please, Nicolas. For me."

Nicolas continued to glare at Retaux. Finally he let go of him. With a disgusted look he turned, stabbing the dagger into the surface of the inlaid table.

"Nicolas."

At Jeanne's severe tone he hastily pulled the dagger free and tucked it away. "Sorry," he said sheepishly.

Retaux leaned back against the window, scanning the street. Jeanne gazed at the two of them and shook her head.

"There can be no more mistakes," she said. "Nicolas—you will not sell diamonds in Paris anymore. Agreed?"

Nicolas poured himself another cognac and downed it with a gulp.

"Say it," Retaux snapped.

Nicolas stared into his glass. Finally, "Agreed," he said.

Retaux turned from the window, his face worn. "We should leave the country while we can. Too much notice has been taken of all of us. Once this affair unravels, Rohan will have our heads staked on his chapel gate."

Jeanne walked to her writing desk and opened a drawer. She hesitated, then took out a bundle of letters bound in violet ribbon. Her face was somber as she turned to the others. "If there is no other recourse left to us, we have the Cardinal's letters to Antoinette."

She slipped the top letter from the pile and held it up to the light. "This one proclaiming his love for the Queen would be particularly damaging."

Nicolas stared at her. His face was pale: until now, not even his escape from the gendarmerie had made him realize the urgency and danger of their situation. "And suppose by that time the Cardinal does not give a Goddamn?" he asked hoarsely.

Jeanne put the letters carefully back into the drawer and locked it. Slowly she walked over to the spinet, where her collection of porcelain angels remained, unmoving, lovely, unalterably calm. She reached to touch the smallest angel, and said, "It will all be fine. We've laid our plans: now we must trust in them."

She picked up the little porcelain figure and cradled it in her palm, her eyes bright but the tears in check, for now: forever, if she had her way.

Chapter

TWENTY-NINE

S o it was that I found myself altering my plans in ways that I had not, at first, intended. Heaven works in such ways, I have been told: and while it may well be that my intentions would not have been sanctioned by Our Lord, I will remind you that I had as my model His shepherd on Earth, Cardinal Rohan. And Rohan's example was such that I believe Satan himself might have learned from him a trick or two. My conscience was not uneasy, then or ever, for engaging in a game of wits with such a wicked man.

In the days and nights that followed I wove a complex web. I wished to ensnare a spider or two, but it was inevitable that more innocent creatures would be trapped. This I know and I beg God's for-giveness for it, but you must ask yourself, have I not paid many times over for my weakness?

I arranged for Monsieur Bohmer to receive an anonymous note, saying that he was the victim of a fraud. This I knew would panic the man, and it did. He immediately summoned his carriage to visit the Cardinal, again as I had hoped. When Bohmer reached the Cardinal with news of the fraud, Rohan would quickly realize his predicament, and in order to avoid scandal, he would be forced to strike a deal with the jeweler. In the event of the Cardinal's rage being diverted to myself and my as-sociates, I still had the Cardinal's damning letters in my possession. I saw no way, in short, that I would be left unprotected.

And History would have proven my plan sound, had not Fortune's pendulum swung the wrong way; had not two carriages met by chance on the King's road, and so brought about my undoing.

Chapter

THIRTY

❧❦

That night Jeanne made her way with as much haste and stealth as she could muster, to the ancient bridge where she had first met Colleen some weeks before. As arranged, the Queen's chambermaid was waiting there. Her pale pinched face revealed how frightened she was; she stepped from the shadows, glancing nervously over her shoulder as she approached Jeanne.

"Listen carefully," the Comtesse commanded. She held out a bundle of envelopes, tied with a red ribbon. "The Cardinal is about to find out that he is the victim of a fraud. When he does, he'll want blood — but he will be told that if any harm comes to us, these love letters that he wrote to Antoinette will find their way to the King. Should anything happen, you are to give these to the House Minister."

Colleen shrank from the proffered bundle. "No! It has all become far too dangerous. I will not be part of this any longer."

She turned to go, but Jeanne grabbed her arm. "Wait."

As Colleen turned reluctantly, Jeanne held up a small but perfect diamond. The chambermaid's eyes widened. "I am sorry to hear that, Colleen. I wanted to properly show you my gratitude for your undertaking this important task."

Colleen swallowed, then nodded. She took the letters and slipped them into her pocket; then let her hand close around the diamond.

"I am your trusted servant, Countess," she said, and hurried back into the shadows.

୬ VERY EARLY THE NEXT MORNING MONSIEUR Bohmer's coach was racketing down the King's highway toward the House of Rohan, with Bohmer inside shouting commands at the driver. He had fortified himself against his visit with copious amounts of Armagnac and snuff; and so when another coach, jet-black and lavishly trimmed with gold, came rushing down the thoroughfare toward him, Bohmer reacted with rather more aplomb than might have ordinarily been his wont.

"Give way, give way!" The round-faced jeweler leaned out his window, pounding on the side of the carriage and nearly tumbling out in the process. "We have important business!"

The driver of the other coach stared at him obdurately, and refused to budge. Monsieur Bohmer fairly jumped from the window, sputtering, "Are you deaf? Give way, I said!"

The driver shrugged. Beneath him, the gilt door of the coach opened slowly. Without haste a tall figure stepped down and into the center of the road, glaring at Monsieur Bohmer. The jeweler blanched, clutching at the window as House Minister Breteuil strode up toward him.

"Minister Breteuil," he stammered, his ruddy face damp with sweat. "What an—an unexpected appearance."

Breteuil stood beside the coach and stared at the jeweler broodingly. He leaned close, sniffing, then grimaced at the smell of brandy. "You have been acting strangely of late, jeweler."

"I—I act no differently than I always have!" protested Bohmer.

"Where are you going in such a hurried fashion?"

Bohmer waved his hands feebly. "I have a pressing engagement with a confidential client."

House Minister Breteuil leaned into the open window of Bohmer's coach and peered around suspiciously. "Urgent rendezvous?" He stared piercingly at Bohmer. "Secretive clientele? I had no idea your position was so fraught with intrigue."

Bohmer swallowed, his eye twitching. "You will never find a more clandestine profession, House Minister! Never!" Bohmer gave the Minister a sickly smile. "I am gratified to have had this chance meeting—perhaps again, sometime soon—"

He started to sink back into his seat, when Breteuil put a hand on the door and opened it. "Ah no—I am fascinated, Monsieur Bohmer. I want to learn more about your exciting profession . . ."

Bohmer's smile went from sickly to downright ill, as the House Minister stepped inside and locked the door behind him.

❧ THE FEAST OF THE ASSUMPTION DAWNED gray and cool, but not even a full-blown thunderstorm could have chilled the Cardinal's spirits as he dressed for Mass that morning. Abel Duphot assisted him at his toilet, holding the petit-point alb that bore the Rohan coat of arms, and slipping it over the Cardinal's crimson soutane as Rohan admired himself in the looking glass. Last of all Duphot climbed onto a velvet footstool and reverently placed the gold-embossed miter atop Rohan's head.

"It makes perfect sense, Your Eminence," he said as he adjusted the miter. "What better occasion than the Feast of the Assumption, to announce your own assumption to the position of Prime Minister?"

Rohan shook his head, still marveling at the thought. "Do you truly think it possible?"

"Why else would the King and Queen summon you in this impromptu manner, when ordinarily Mass would not be said until this evening?"

Rohan drew himself to his full height, raising his arms to display the yards of lush fabric that made his robes. "It is indeed a historic day for the House of Rohan," he said with pride.

"Extremely historic, Your Eminence."

Rohan turned back and forth in front of the looking glass, examining himself from every possible angle. Satisfied at last, he strode toward the door of his dressing room, but before leaving he paused. Abel Duphot hurried to his side, frowning.

"Is something wrong, Your Eminence?"

Rohan stroked his chin. "Nothing should mar this day for me. I want my mind and conscience to be free and clear, to enjoy what my courage has earned for my lineage."

He gazed down at Abel Duphot with an expression of the utmost seriousness. "There is one last thing which we must do," he announced, then turned and left the room.

❧ FEAST DAY OR NOT, THE HALL OF MIRRORS at Versailles was filled as ever with its noisy, pandering, backbiting crowd of aristocrats and hangers-on, all mingling and gossiping as they awaited the arrival of the King and Queen. Outside, pale sunlight broke through the clouds but was quickly overtaken by the patter of cold rain; inside, however, the Hall glowed with the light from a thousand reflected candles.

Within this gala atmosphere, the Countess de La Motte-Valois and her handsome husband were themselves more welcome than ever before. News of the Countess's friendship with the Queen had raced through the court, and ever since Jeanne had found herself at the center of a circle of admirers. Now she moved gracefully among courtiers and elegant women, demurely fending off compliments and invitations to dine as she sought out her husband, himself surrounded by a quartet of simpering women.

"Nicolas?" she called in a low voice, smiling coquettishly. "Do recall that we have a meeting arranged for a short time from now . . ."

Nicolas gave a gallant bow to the women. "Excuse me," he said, kissing the hand of one particularly well-dressed young lady. "The Countess needs my advice on a matter that will not wait."

He joined her, and when they were out of sight of the others whispered, "Are you certain that you want to face Rohan here, my dear?"

He nodded toward the end of the hall. Cardinal Rohan and his secretary were just making their entrance, the Cardinal striding purposefully toward the very spot where Jeanne and Nicolas stood. Jeanne smiled automatically at a passing gentleman, then took her husband's arm. "We must deal with His Eminence at some point," she said, steeling herself as Rohan drew near them. "At least here, in this crowd, he is less likely to cause a scene—"

She drew herself upright as Rohan came within a few feet of them. To her astonishment, he smiled at her benignly, nodded, and went on.

Nicolas raised his eyebrows, turning to watch the Cardinal disappear into the passage leading to the King's private chambers. "That was not *quite* the reaction I expected," he said.

"Nor I," said Jeanne with an uneasy frown. "Nor I."

THE CARDINAL'S DAYDREAMS OF TRIUMPH were as fleeting as the sun that had momentarily ignited the gardens outside Versailles. He had scarcely had a full minute to himself in the King's private study, preening before a portrait of Antoinette, when Louis, the Queen, and House Minister Breteuil burst in upon him with evidence of perfidy, in the form of a written statement from Monsieur Bohmer.

King Louis, as always, was uncomfortable. He fidgeted like a child, until Antoinette gave him a sharp look that sent him scuttling off to a corner where he idly spun a large globe and listened to Breteuil's accusations.

"May I ask under what conditions this statement was made?" Rohan stood in the center of the chamber and scanned Bohmer's document, his arrogance undiminished.

"A verbal interrogation here at the palace," replied Breteuil. "It lasted all of one minute. Then Monsieur Bohmer gushed forth what he knew like a ruptured water gut."

The King poked the globe with his forefinger, stopping it. He looked pained as he turned to the Cardinal and asked, "Do you deny your participation in this affair?"

Rohan's eyes flashed, but he only said, "No, Your Majesty."

House Minister Breteuil stepped beside the King. He pointed at the document in the Cardinal's hand. "Do you disagree with anything in the court jeweler's statement?"

"I do not."

Louis glanced at his wife, then asked querulously, "Then you admit that you used the Queen's good name to acquire this necklace for your own gain?"

"I most vehemently deny that, Your Majesty!" cried Rohan.

Antoinette gazed at Rohan with undisguised contempt. "How could you believe that I would choose you to act as my emissary with the court jewelers? You, to whom I have not addressed a single word in nearly ten years?"

Embarrassed, the Cardinal looked from the Queen to her husband. At last his gaze settled on Antoinette. "Do you not remember, Your Majesty—?"

He made a show of giving her the same formal nod he had been met with in the Grove of Venus. The Queen stared at him, bewildered and angry, as the Cardinal's gaze shifted to her portrait on the wall. Once again, he turned back to her and, very carefully, nodded.

"Is there something wrong with your neck, Monsieur?" demanded Antoinette.

The King looked at Rohan with distaste. "Your behavior indicates a familiarity with the Queen which I find offensive. Leave us."

The Cardinal began to protest, then stopped. He turned and gazed at the portrait, an unpleasant possibility suddenly beginning to stir his thoughts. Quickly he whirled and addressed the Queen.

"Your Majesty! I beseech you—out of consideration for my family, and the centuries of service which we have rendered unto you—please, keep this matter between us until—"

The House Minister shook his head. "The King has given his instructions," he said icily.

"No!" The Cardinal turned desperately to Antoinette. "You must hear me out! That Countess, Jeanne de La Motte—"

Breteuil stepped between them. "Leave the chamber, Cardinal Rohan."

Rohan gave a last anguished look at the Queen. Then he bowed and hurried from the room. As soon as he was gone Antoinette turned on the others.

"That viper has used my name like a clumsy counterfeiter!" she cried. "He has debased not only my name, but the entire reputation of the monarchy!"

Dismayed by his wife's outburst, Louis rocked back and forth on his heels. Finally he looked at Breteuil. "House Minister? Your thoughts on the matter?"

Breteuil shrugged. "Despite the Cardinal's considerable personal fortune, he does incur staggering debts. This may well have been a ploy to pay off his creditors."

"Do you think he would try to leave the country?"

The slightest of smiles creased the House Minister's face. "If I were in his position, Your Majesty, I would."

Antoinette's face tightened. She crossed to the

door, stood there for a moment before delivering her final pronouncement. "Our course on this is clear. House Minister, I leave it in your hands," she said, and with a steely look at Breteuil she left.

Chapter

THIRTY-ONE

❧❧

In the Hall of Mirrors, Jeanne and Nicolas stood
chatting with a group of courtiers, when the
bang of a door closing echoed through the great
space. Several people tittered. Nicolas looked up
sharply, then touched his wife's wrist.

"It's time we take our leave," he said in a low
voice, inclining his head. Jeanne glanced where he
indicated and saw Cardinal Rohan storming out of
the passage to the King's chambers. He pushed his
way past a knot of curious onlookers, saw Jeanne,
and shouted.

"Stay where you are, Countess!"

"Jeanne, we must go," urged Nicolas.

But Jeanne held her ground. The courtiers who

moments before had been so amused by her conversation backed away, being careful to remain within hearing distance. The Cardinal swept past them, reaching out to snatch her by the wrist; but before his hand closed around her he was seized from behind by one of the King's guard.

"What manner of insult is this?" the Cardinal roared. He turned, crimson with rage, and found himself face to face with Breteuil.

"The King has ordered your arrest," announced the House Minister.

The Cardinal stared at him in disbelief. "That can't be!"

"I advise you not to make a scene, Your Eminence," Breteuil said calmly. He made a discreet hand gesture to the remaining guards, who surrounded Rohan and began escorting him from the hall. The Cardinal struggled against them, pointing toward the door.

"She is the one you want!" he cried. "The Countess de La Motte—"

Breteuil turned but saw only a throng of gaping courtiers, excitedly vying with each other to witness the Cardinal's disgrace.

Chapter

THIRTY-TWO

A hard gray rain slanted against the narrow windows of Château de La Motte. Inside, flames danced merrily within the massive stone fireplace, belying the weather outside and the somber expression on the face of the Comtesse where she sat, staring into the blaze.

"Jeanne."

She drew a hand across her face and looked up. In the doorway stood Retaux, his cloak dripping onto the stone floor and his dark hair plastered to his forehead.

"I rode all afternoon." He stepped into the room, tossed his cloak over a chair, then crossed to stand beside her. "And I heard news before I left Paris. Rohan has been sent to the Bastille."

Jeanne's gaze never left the fire. "Rest assured, his cell will be the best they have to offer."

Retaux placed his hands on her shoulder, wincing as he felt Jeanne flinch at his touch. "He has most certainly implicated us. Jeanne, you *must* listen to me—any time now, they could—"

"I do not intend to leave." Her gaze hardened, and she moved imperceptibly away from him. "After all these years, the name *Valois* is once again spoken with respect. I will not diminish my family's honor by running away."

"To fiery hell with the name!" Retaux flung his hands up and stalked in front of the fireplace. "It will do you little good in the King's prison!"

Jeanne jumped to her feet and stared at him fiercely. "Then go, Retaux! I have not asked you to stay!"

Retaux turned to her. "Please tell me, Madame," he said, and his voice was soft with pain, "that conspiracy was not all that held us together . . ."

Jeanne shook her head, tears welling in her eyes. "Save yourself, Retaux. I want you to."

"And who will protect you if I go?" he demanded. "Nicolas? If it comes to it, he will give you up to save himself! You know that, Jeanne!"

"You need not concern yourself with Nicolas."

She turned away. Retaux frowned, looking at her closely, then tenderly took her chin in his hand.

Once more he could feel her flinch at his touch, but after a moment she relaxed, and let him gently turn her face toward the firelight.

He sucked his breath in. A violet bruise bloomed across her cheek, and from her lower lip a fine seam of blood ran down to her chin. His face contorted with fury, Retaux lifted his head to the ceiling and shouted.

"Nicolas!"

He let go of her and started to run into the next room, but when he reached the door he halted. On a table there lay the red leather case, tossed into the corner.

It was empty. Retaux turned to Jeanne. Her eyes met his and she nodded.

"He has taken his leave."

With a strangled cry Retaux lunged for the front door. Jeanne grabbed him, shouting, "Let him go! Retaux, let him —"

He pushed her away and she fell, hard, against the table. Retaux let out a moan and leaned against the wall, then reached for her. "Jeanne. Oh, God, please —"

"Stay away!" she screamed, kicking at him. *"Don't touch me!"*

Retaux buried his head in his hands, then looked up. "Jeanne. Please. You must not remain here. Come away with me. Now."

She shook her head, refusing to meet his gaze. Retaux stared at her, pleading. When still she would not look at him or answer, he cried, "For God's sake! What is there in a name that is worth your life? Tell me, Jeanne, for I cannot see the reason!"

A long minute passed when neither of them said a word. Then, slowly, Jeanne raised her face to stare at him, and said, "It only matters that I see it."

In her eyes there was nothing of love or remorse, nothing of their history or passion; only that hard cold inward gaze. Retaux closed his eyes, letting out a cry of pain and futile rage. Then in a frenzy he turned. He grabbed his cloak and flung it over himself, then dashed back out into the rain.

Jeanne let him go. After a few minutes she walked to the open door, stood there, and watched as Retaux stumbled through the slashing rain to where a stable boy stood holding the traces of his horse. Without a word he took the reins from the boy and swung up into the saddle. For one last time he stared across the courtyard at Jeanne. Then he dug his heels into the horse's flanks, and with a wordless cry galloped off into the storm.

She remained there, silent and unmoving, the rain slashing her face and the wind lifting her hair in dank strands. When at last she turned and went back inside the fire had died to embers. As though she were one of Cagliostro's sleepwalkers, she walked slowly around the room, taking first the red leather case and then a stack of gilt-edged stationery, and bearing all of these to the fireplace. Then she knelt there, heedless of the ash and old

cinders biting into her knees, tossed the case and
heavy paper onto the embers and watched as the
fire blazed up once more, consigning them all to the
flames.

⤴ HE CAUGHT UP WITH NICOLAS ON THE
King's southern highway, the thoroughfare that led
to the nearest port from which one could escape to
England. The rain had grown to a torrent, sluicing
down the rutted road and filling the ditches with
water the color of dirty cream, and the roar of rushing water drowned out all other noises. When Retaux came up behind him Nicolas heard nothing
but rain.

"You son of a bitch!" Retaux's rapier slashed
through the air, but Nicolas was already away, his
horse dashing toward the woods. Retaux followed,
shouting. At the edge of the road Nicolas spurred
his mount around, drawing his own sword.

"Come on, you coward! I'll meet you face-on!"

The riders clashed, the ringing of their swords
lost beneath the raging storm. Nicolas's blade sliced
through Retaux's cloak. Blood mingled with the
rain streaming down his arm, but Retaux parried
Nicolas's next thrust, grabbing his cape and leaping
from his own horse so that he could drag Nicolas to
the ground after him. Nicolas kicked at him, and together they crashed into the underbrush. Retaux

struggled to get to his feet as Nicolas stumbled past him, heading for the road and turning to brandish his sword in Retaux's face. With a shout Retaux ducked, then kicked Nicolas squarely in the face. The count went flying backward. As he did, a leather pouch flew from his jacket, landing on a patch of bracken. Starlit fragments scattered across the moss and ferns: all that remained of the Queen's necklace. Nicolas gave an anguished cry, rolling onto his stomach and reaching frantically for them. Retaux stood above him, panting, as Nicolas stared wildly at the jewels.

"She is incapable of trust!" he shouted at his wife's lover. "She cannot trust! And without her trust, you will never be more than a useful object to her! I learned that, but you never did, you ass!"

Retaux kicked him brutally in the stomach. Nicolas screamed as his ribs cracked. "You know nothing about us!" Retaux shouted into the driving rain. "Nothing!"

Nicolas rolled over, coughing. Blood spattered the green bracken as Retaux grabbed him by the throat and began to squeeze. Nicolas's struggles quieted; his breath came in short gasps. He blinked, his eyes streaming from the rain, and saw through a haze of red and gray the glitter of diamonds on the moss a few feet away. Feebly his hands moved, striving to reach them.

"Sweet Christ," said Retaux in disgust. He relaxed his grip, and Nicolas inhaled raggedly, coughing as he began to drag himself through the mud and crushed undergrowth, still struggling to reach the diamonds. Retaux turned away and lurched back toward his horse. Blood seeped through his shirt and breeches, but he paid it no heed; he only swung himself onto his horse and spurred it back onto the road.

Chapter

THIRTY-THREE

❧❦

There was one thing left for me to do. The rain had not slackened, but I no longer cared; nor did I feel its chill bite as I walked, bareheaded, away from the château. Perhaps a half-mile from our home the road forks and the right-hand curve begins to descend into the village. This was the road I followed. I passed no one save a family of peasants sitting dull-eyed in a donkey cart, the cart trundling through the rain no faster than my own footsteps. They turned blankly curious faces to me, but I had no care. I knew where I had to go, and nothing would keep me from my journey.

The cemetery in that village is bound by iron gates, rusted from neglect, the headstones within furred with moss and weeds and cracked from the passage of many winter snows. I had not been there for years upon years, yet I knew the way as though I had walked it each night in my sleep: which, indeed, I had. My fingers closed around the little angel necklace I had purchased on that last happy afternoon with Retaux in Paris. The necklace I had thought would be a talisman, to bring me luck; as I had thought Retaux would bring me luck, by virtue of his love for me, his passion and his loyalty. None of those things, I now know, promises fortune. Nothing does.

For a long time I stood there by the gate. At last I pushed it open, hesitating, then stepped over the threshold. As I did I saw before me another day, snow on the ground and not rain, and to either side of me the figures of the Marquis and Marquise Boullainvillers, comforting me who would never again know the meaning of comfort, or peace.

"Control yourself, child!"

The Marquis' voice rang out loudly among the tombstones as I pulled away from them and threw myself onto the ground. I was sobbing so hard that I choked; when the Marquis reached out to soothe me I struck at him violently.

"No, Jeanne!" his wife cried in dismay, as I rolled and began scratching at my own face. She dropped to her knees beside me, the dirty snow staining her elegant fur cloak, and enfolded me in her arms. "My dear child, calm yourself—there, my darling, there—"

She held me to her breast, stroking my head until the fit passed. Still I sobbed, gasping as I tried to speak. "I—I could not keep her warm enough! I tried, but it was so cold at night. It's my fault! It's my fault—"

"Oh, my poor dear," the Marquise crooned, rocking me back and forth. "You must not blame yourself—you too are only a child—"

"I was her sister!" I tried to pull away from her. "She relied on me—"

But the Marquise would not let me go. She held onto me firmly but with great tenderness, and said, "Who can know God's reasoning? Perhaps her purpose was to keep *you* warm, so that you might live. Think of her warmth as her gift to you."

A shadow fell across us. The Marquis stood looking down, nodding at his wife and then at me. "If that be the case, child, you owe it to your sister to make something of yourself. Don't you think?"

I gazed up at him, his words resounding in my ears, then nodded. "Yes," I said, my voice a whisper. "Yes . . ."

Later, after the last spadefuls of earth had been tossed onto her grave, I knelt there alone, my cheek against the cold marble headstone that the Marquis had paid for. "My innocent sister," I whispered, staring up at the carved stone figure of an angel, its features those of my beloved sister, its calm wide eyes her eyes. "For your death to have meaning, my life must be remarkable . . ."

". . . my life must be remarkable," I said aloud, all those years later, as I knelt once more beside her. I pressed my forehead against the cold marble and let my tears fall as they had so long ago, mingling with the rain beneath my knees.

That was how they found me. I heard the muted thud of hooves upon the path leading to the grave-yard then the creak and groan of the iron gate opening.

"Jeanne de La Motte-Valois?"

I lifted my head to see the tall broad figure of House Minister Breteuil standing there in the rain, the cowl of his cloak falling back as he stepped to-ward me. Behind him three members of the local gendarmerie waited alongside a donkey cart where three round-faced peasants sat, watching me through slitted eyes. I looked from them to the Min-ister, then with all the composure I could muster stood, smoothing the damp hair from my face and tilting my head proudly as I nodded in reply.

"Yes, Monsieur. You have the honor."

And I let them escort me from that place, saying not a word as I walked down the road past my fam-ily home, and bade it a silent farewell.

Chapter

THIRTY-FOUR

～❧❧～

In a set of heavily curtained rooms hidden deep within the city of Paris, a sorcerer manqué and his manservant moved silently but efficiently amid the tapestries and lavish furniture, packing a large valise with clothes, gold and silver goblets, a small jewel-box, brocade wallets stuffed with money and documents. When they were finished, Cagliostro hurriedly threw an immense black cape over his shoulders, pulling it to cover his face.

Then he strode to the door. Unexpectedly he stopped, turned to pull a small painting from the wall, and hid it beneath his cloak. Then he followed his servant out the door, leaving the room empty behind him.

Chapter

THIRTY-FIVE

❧

The Bastille held the Comtesse de La Motte now, as well as Cardinal Rohan. The city, too, was tight in an iron grasp—that of winter. Snow blanketed the streets; the citizens of Paris stumbled through the drifts to market, fighting for the little bread there was to be had and then staggering home again, to shiver before graying embers and comfort themselves and their children as best they could.

Snow did not distress Antoinette overmuch. One of the palace's gilded sledges bore her through the icy streets; she sat enshrouded in a sable cape trimmed with ermine, Madame Campan across from her and the two of them laughing, their cheeks ablaze from the chill.

"Isn't it lovely!" cried the Queen. She lifted a gloved hand and watched a stray flake fall upon her palm. "It's like in Austria, a real winter . . ."

In front of the royal sleigh veered a hay wagon, its wheels straining and buckling in the snowdrifts. Antoinette's sledge slowed nearly to a stop. She looked around uneasily, as ragged citizens clambered atop the mounds of dirty snow and stared at her.

"Rohan's whore!" a woman shouted, her face contorted with hatred.

"Going to the Cardinal now, are you?" another cried. "Thieves of a kind, the two of you!"

A crowd was gathering. Madame Campan called urgently to the driver, who swore at the hay wagon's driver; but the sledge did not move. A beggar pushed his way to the top of a heap of snow filthy with ashes, opened his arms beseechingly to Antoinette and shouted, "Ah, throw us a brilliant, my sweet! Any odd diamond will do!"

The crowd laughed. "Here's a diamond for you!" someone cried, as a snowball smashed against the sleigh. Antoinette's driver lashed the horses furiously. With a screech the sleigh's runners tore through slush and ice and the hay wagon canted dangerously to the left, as the Queen's sledge raced past.

"Clearly the situation is not improving!" Antoinette exclaimed indignantly, staring back at the rabble screaming curses at her. "It is quite the opposite!"

She was still seething that night when she met with Breteuil in her husband's study. "I think that now only one action can set this right," she said, pacing anxiously back and forth. Louis and the House Minister exchanged worried looks as she went on. "The case must be tried in open Parliament."

Breteuil shook his head. "That would be a grave mistake, Your Majesty. It is within the King's right to pass judgment on this matter. Why place it in less sympathetic hands?"

"Because the King's word is worth little to the people now," Antoinette snapped. "They respect only the judgment of Parliament. The only way that my name will be absolved is if Parliament convicts Rohan as the sole perpetrator of the crime."

"And if they acquit him?" said Louis. "Won't that be tantamount to saying that you were guilty?"

Antoinette walked angrily past him. Breteuil approached her and said, "His Majesty is correct. You could not be tried, of course, but the guilt will fall upon you all the same."

The Queen crossed to the window, refusing to look at either of them. She stared out to where snow blew in deceptively peaceful eddies, and tugged peevishly at the ringlets framing her face.

"Public vindication, House Minister." Her expression was unyielding. "I will accept nothing less."

She turned and swept from the room. The King sighed, fiddling with a clock on his desk. "Your thoughts, House Minister?" he asked.

House Minister Breteuil gazed at him with sober eyes. "The Queen offers up a sweet plum before ravens," he said in a deeply worried tone. "Pray none of them takes a bite — or devours it whole."

Chapter

THIRTY-SIX

If it could be said that the Cardinal had little influence with the Queen, I had even less with House Minister Breteuil. Our arrests created a torrent of rumor. Wagons full of broadsheets stood at every corner, providing the good citizens of Paris with what they hungered for more than even bread or wine: the scandal du jour, a feast that changed daily, and for which no one's appetite ever seemed to diminish. One popular story being circulated suggested that the Queen and Cardinal Rohan had acted in concert to obtain the necklace. Another story insinuated that the Queen was carrying Rohan's illegitimate child. I, too, had my part to play in this ever-changing melodrama. In one account, I was portrayed as a cunning opportunist. In another, I was seen as an unwilling pawn.

Still, no matter my role in this theatrical, I did not earn the comforts that were the Cardinal's by right as a Prince of Rohan. My quarters at the Bastille were grim, a small cell with only a pallet on the floor and slop for refreshment. Rosalie was allowed me as a companion. She would have starved in the streets otherwise during that wolf winter, with no family in Paris and no employer.

Rohan, though, might almost have imagined he had taken up residence in a disused but serviceable wing of his own palace. His chambers took up an entire floor of one of the Bastille's smaller wings; he was permitted servants and visitors, including Madame de Niess, whose appearance of youthful innocence did not preclude her from adding to the Cardinal's creature comforts. There was a balcony outside of Rohan's quarters, and Rosalie and I often saw him there, taking the winter air before retiring to write more missives to the Queen pleading his innocence and decrying myself as a witch and wanton.

Those were strange days, in which Cardinal Rohan and I found ourselves reluctant neighbors in the cold vast confines of the Bastille. There were others, too, who had the misfortune to be implicated—the tiny white-faced child known as the Dove, whom Rosalie comforted as though she were her own child. And one day while outside I witnessed the arrival of a carriage thundering across the fortress drawbridge. A score of mounted gendarmes followed, so that I thought this must be a very dangerous prisoner indeed, perhaps the instigator Camille Desmoulins, or one of those who were rumored to be plotting the overthrow of the throne.

But when the carriage door opened, I recognized the figure that emerged: tall, black-clad, arrogant even now: his hauteur armoring him more effectively than any mail. As he stepped down a guard attempted to grab his arm, but Cagliostro only hissed at him, raising his hand with two fingers extended in an evil manner, so that the guard fell back cowering and the gendarmes shrank from him as he marched through the great entrance hall and into the fortress.

There were rumors within the Bastille, as well. One day Rosalie and I heard that the Queen had had a change of heart, and I was to be pardoned; that very night news reached me that I would be brought to the gallows at dawn. Neither scene played out within our dark theater; nor did the grand finale featuring Rohan's escape, Cagliostro's disappearance in a ball of flame, or my own death at the hands of a paid assassin.

And yet a day dawned when I found myself once more a player in the great drama that was Paris, not merely a prisoner. My breakfast was as usual thin cold porridge, but after the bowl was taken from me another guard appeared behind the door grate.

"You are to dress yourself in traveling clothes, Madame," he said respectfully. "You will be escorted from here in an hour's time, to face the judgment of Parliament."

How to explain to you the sense I felt, an hour and a half later, when the carriage that bore me from the Bastille reached the steps of the Palais de Justice? In the months of my confinement I had imagined often my removal from that terrible place; but never had I dared dream of the crowds that greeted me on the palace steps. I was surprised and not a little frightened at the sight of so many people gathered there, and quite frankly terrified as I disembarked from the coach, lest they set upon me and kill me there in the street. Those were terrible days, you must recall, and more than one citizen had fallen victim to mob justice and ended with his head on a pike, rotting along a boulevard for all to spit upon.

But what greeted me was not rage but approbation: at sight of me the crowd roared with excitement and delight, and one woman ran forward to thrust a bouquet of withered violets into my hand.

"God keep you!" she cried, before the guards pulled her away.

It seems that amid the confusion and exaggerations surrounding the scandal of the Queen's necklace, I had emerged as a champion of the people! Like themselves, they saw me as a victim, subjected to the greedy whims and sly machinations of the aristocracy. Fearful that they would see me freed by the throng, the guards rushed me up the steps and into the Palais de Justice, a place I had often passed by but where I had never set foot. The halls were no less crowded than the courtyard outside, but here was no ragged populace, but a black-robed army of clerks and assistants to the members of Parliament. They stared at me with open curiosity, and some with what looked very like pity; but no one said a word to me until I was in the Grand Chamber.

It was a cold, cheerless place. Light spilled down from high clerestory windows, but the effect was not warming but rather that of having a lantern thrust into your face, leaving no shadow or corner in which to find refuge. The thirty-four judges of Parliament sat in rows of dark walnut benches, their red robes and white periwigs the only notes of color in that somber room. Behind a desk on a raised dais, President d'Aligre sat flanked by Magistrate Titon and Magistrate de Marce, all three of them black-robed, and no more reassuring than the ranks of judges behind them. Opposite them sat Abel Duphot and Cardinal Rohan, staring at me hatefully from their bench. House Minister Breteuil sat beside them, his expression unreadable.

"Jeanne de La Motte-Valois," President d'Aligre began in stentorian tones. "We have assembled here this day to bring judgment on you and the other defendants in this matter, as instructed by His Majesty, Louis XVI."

I stood before him proudly, my hood revealing enough of my face to pique the interest of those assembled. They were, after all, men; and I was interested to note that, like those outside, many of the faces that met me here were not unkind, and many were pitying.

"I trust that your stay at the Bastille was tolerable, Madame?" President d'Aligre asked in a gentler tone.

"I did not have to be torn from its bosom," I replied coolly, and heard a rustle of laughter pass through the room. "Indeed, my accommodations were meager compared to those of Cardinal Rohan. Why, one day he entertained a party of thirty men, who feasted with him on oysters and champagne. I understand some of you were in attendance," I added as the laughter died and the judges stirred uncomfortably on their benches.

"Countess," President d'Aligre interjected sternly. "Before a reading of the record of your interrogations, do you care to make remarks to the judging body?"

I lowered the hood of my cape, turning to regard first one side of the chamber, and then the other. Cardinal Rohan and his secretary exchanged a look. "Though I have been shrouded in the Bastille," I said, hoping my voice would not betray my fear, "I am aware of powerful forces at work against me. In the face of these hostilities, I will endeavour to defend myself with a strong feminine logic."

I looked at House Minister Breteuil. "I urge each of you not to succumb to outside pressures. Act as true sentinels of justice, defending the honor of the French people."

I crossed the room, stopping before a bench and speaking slowly and with great emotion.

"In my own defense, I will say only this. If I reached for anything that shone brilliantly, it was the vision of a home denied me, and a sense of peace I had never known — not since my childhood, when it was torn from me. I wanted my life to be as it should have been. In the eyes of God, and the world, that can be no crime."

I turned and walked back to my bench and began to sit but stopped. I gazed up at President d'Aligre, waiting for him to acknowledge me. It took a moment, but then he rose from his chair and inclined his head to me, as one does to indicate respect for a woman of note. He glanced aside, clearing his throat, until one by one the other members of Parliament followed suit. I waited until the last venerable man had gotten to his feet, and then with great dignity I sat. I could feel d'Aligre's eyes on me, and when I glanced aside I saw him staring at me with a half-smile on his august face.

The Parliamentary President, it seemed, could appreciate and admire a woman's spirit.

The testimony of the others, however, did not proceed quickly or without rancor. Nothing, though, could have prepared me for the unpleasant experience of standing beside Cardinal Rohan in the center of the chamber, while Magistrate Titon accused me of the most base crimes.

"The Cardinal suggests that you were in collusion with Cagliostro," he said, jabbing a finger in the air.

I tossed my head. "I despise the man and the Count feels the same toward me. Hardly an ideal mix for conspirators."

"That was a ruse to hide your true intent," countered Rohan.

The Magistrate nodded. "The child known as the Dove—she is the daughter of your maidservant Rosalie, is she not?"

"She is a motherless orphan whom we befriended in the Bastille!" I protested. "Thrown there at the Cardinal's bequest—"

Magistrate Titon picked up a document from the table before him and held it up to the President. "I have documentation here that says otherwise. Cardinal?"

Rohan pointed to another paper. "Not long after I relinquished the necklace to the Countess, Cagliostro appeared at a brokerage. My investigators learned that he sold the owner four large diamonds of quality."

President d'Aligre turned. For the first time I saw Cagliostro, seated between two guards on a bench at the very back of the room. "Count Cagliostro, have you anything to say on your own behalf?"

Even from across the room I could feel his gaze searing mine. I looked away quickly, as he stood and walked to the center of the table. There he remained for some moments, fixing each of the Parliamentarians in turn with his piercing stare.

"I have called upon my considerable memory," he said at last, purring as though he spoke seductive words to a woman, and not his own defense. "And no, I can think of no misdeed to account for my arrest. Unless of course it might be the assassination of Pompey in the third century—although I must say that, as regards that particular antique crime, I acted only upon the Pharaoh's orders."

The judges laughed out loud. I stole a quick look at Cagliostro, and he nodded at me very slightly. President d'Aligre raised a hand to silence the Parliament, as Cardinal Rohan railed.

"How do you explain your trip to the brokerage house, then?"

Cagliostro wrinkled his nose, as though he were suppressing a sneeze. From his pocket he withdrew a handkerchief of indigo silk, flicking it open and then sneezing into it. He drew the handkerchief from his face, gazing into it with mock astonishment; he then walked over to the Cardinal, tipped up the handkerchief, and poured four large diamonds into Rohan's open palm.

Once more the Judges laughed, and Cagliostro stared haughtily at Rohan. "I hardly need a disreputable Countess to produce a few stones."

I dipped my head, smiling, as the Cardinal shot me a murderous look. He looked down at the gems in his hand, bent to place one on the floor and stomped on it. It shattered into gray dust.

"Glass!" he cried triumphantly. "Do you see? Trickery is his only gift, and he used it in concert with Jeanne de La Motte to manipulate me!"

"Cardinal Rohan, he must have proof of your charges." President d'Aligre shook his head. "Can you provide any tangible evidence?"

"The letters from the Queen," the Cardinal said. "The Countess forged them, somehow."

"Produce them then."

For a blinding moment I stood there, holding my breath; then saw the Cardinal staring at me. At last he turned away.

"I am unable to do so," he said.

Surprised murmurs passed between the judges. President d'Aligre raised his eyebrows. "How then are you to expect us to believe in the truth of what you say?"

"It was the day of the Feast of the Assumption." Rohan turned his cold eyes upon me, but I would not avert my gaze. "The day when this horror began. I was in my private salon, preparing myself for the Mass of the Assumption. My secretary, Monsieur Duphot, was with me." Abel Duphot gave a slight nod, and the Cardinal went on. "Monsieur Duphot has served me well for many years. He knows the importance of—reticence, in certain private matters, especially as regards one who holds my esteemed position in our Holy Mother Church. We take sacred vows, and these often require that we maintain silence—"

"As in matters pertaining to the confessional?" prompted d'Aligre.

"That is correct. I had secreted the letters I received from Her Majesty. These are unruly times, as the esteemed members of Parliament here today will certainly agree . . ."

Mutters of assent, as Rohan tilted his head toward the President. "Under the circumstances, I felt the letters might be damaging to an already vulnerable monarchy. In addition, I believed that I had obtained the Prime Ministership and wished to protect my benefactress from any scandal. So I ordered the letters burned."

At these words I could not help but relax somewhat, although I was aware of President d'Aligre's stare upon me, indeed the gaze of every member of Parliament—observing me, to determine some sign of guilt. I kept my own eyes downcast as the Cardinal said, "It was only after my arrest that I realized I had destroyed the only evidence that could clear my name. If I could be allowed time to gather additional—"

House Minister Breteuil rose from his chair. "Of all the things that you possess, Cardinal, time is not one of them." He glanced at the President. "May I?"

D'Aligre nodded. "The court recognizes House Minister Breteuil."

My heart began to pound as Breteuil approached me. "It would seem that you and Cagliostro have carried the day, Countess," he said smoothly. "The Cardinal has employed all of his considerable resources, and proved absolutely nothing."

Rohan scowled at Breteuil. I felt another momentary pulse of relief, but then Breteuil turned, nodding at a guard near an anteroom door, and added, "Though Cardinal Rohan would perceive me as a potential enemy, in the near future he may well have cause to thank me . . ."

The door opened. My flesh turned to ice as a veiled woman walked demurely into the chamber. Her head was bowed but her features were unmistakable to me, and to every man in that room, as I heard a single name whispered throughout the gallery.

"Antoinette . . ."

I kept my head down, but even so Breteuil noted my discomposure. "Did you presume that while you sat idle in the Bastille I was idle as well, Countess?"

He motioned the woman to come to the center of the room. As she passed me, I noticed that beneath her plum velvet dress her belly swelled, straining against the expensive fabric.

"Your veil, please," said President d'Aligre.

With an obedient nod she drew the veil from her face. There was a sudden audible intake of breath within the room, as every man there gasped, turning to his neighbor in amazement. Rohan too looked taken aback, but also, for the first time, hopeful. House Minister Breteuil turned to him, gesturing at the new witness.

"Cardinal Rohan, is this the woman you encountered in the Grove of Venus?"

"Yes! Yes, I'm certain of it!"

Breteuil nodded and turned back to the woman. "Mademoiselle, state your name, please."

"Nicole Leguay d'Oliva," she said in a sweet, clear voice. I could sense the members of Parliament restraining themselves: not just her features, but her very voice, were those of the Queen. "Oliva is a name given to me by the Countess. A name I have carried since the beginning of our term of business together."

Magistrate de Marce stood, no longer able to remain still. "Mademoiselle! How was it that you entered into this arrangement with the Countess?"

Nicole gave a simpering smile. "I was in the Park Royal, with my little darlings—my little dogs. We had just been to the patisserie, and I was feeding them bits of cake—the owner of the patisserie is very fond of me and my dogs. It was there that I was approached by the Count de La Motte—"

She looked at me and nodded, her blue eyes wide as a child's. "*Her* husband. At first I was alarmed by his request. The Count, however, was persuasive and extremely charming each time he encountered me in the park."

"Each time?" President d'Aligre frowned. "I am perplexed that a woman of your grace and demeanor would ever be seen in such a common place."

Nicole smiled again: slyly, this time. "The Park Royal suits my needs quite well."

Snide chuckles and leers from some of the judges. President d'Aligre picked up his gavel and silenced them, then turned to Breteuil. "House Minister, thank you for the testimony of your witness. In the best interest of this court and those whom it serves, I call an adjournment to this case until tomorrow morning at ten of the clock."

The judges waited as the guards approached me first of all those accused, and led me back to the Bastille. I knew then that it would not go well with me, but if I could only with difficulty maintain my innocence, my dignity I would not discard too easily: my gaze as I met the eyes of all those assembled—the judges, the President and magistrates, Rohan and Breteuil and Cagliostro and last of all the betrayer Nicole d'Oliva—my gaze was that of a daughter of the House of Valois, valiant and proud to the last.

The unhappy task of submitting Nicole d'O-
liva's testimony to Her Majesty fell, as did
most unhappy tasks, to House Minister Breteuil. He
found her backstage at the tiny jewel-box theater in
the Petit Trianon, wearing pasty theatrical makeup
and the costume laces and bows of a virgin goddess.

"Your Majesty . . ." Breteuil glanced around to
where actors and a coterie of young dancers raced
about backstage, stumbling into each other amid
buffets of laughter: this week's troupe of favorites,
culled from the *Comedie Francaise.* "It would appear
that the woman who impersonated you was, among
other things . . ."

He hesitated, then said, ". . . known to traffic in her charms."

Antoinette stared at him in disbelief. "A *prostitute*?"

He nodded regretfully.

"Has this become public?"

Once more Breteuil paused before answering. "I'm afraid it has. The news sheets are having their way with it."

Antoinette's painted face collapsed into a sullen mask. She slowly lowered herself onto a flimsy love seat that was part of the stage set. A minute passed before she spoke again.

"Rohan and Countess de La Motte must suffer for this." She fixed Breteuil with a severe look. "Do not fail me, Breteuil."

"It will be as you wish, Your Majesty," he said, and bowing, took his leave.

THE PARLIAMENT RECONVENED THE NEXT morning as appointed. I had passed a troubled night, having told a tearful Rosalie that despite my best intentions she and her accused child would, after all, be left friendless upon their release from the Bastille. As to my own fate, I did not dare project my thoughts that far. I saw only darkness, and since childhood I have feared the night.

In the Grand Chamber Rohan and I stood behind the railing that faced the raised dais, the two of us taking care not to meet each other's eyes. The House Minister was in conference with President d'Aligre. I did not have to see Rohan to sense his agitation: not all his luxurious robes and vestments could keep him from imprisonment, and even the grandest apartments in the Bastille would make a cold homecoming.

I did not want to imagine where I might lay my head.

"Countess de La Motte." I looked up, startled; sleeplessness and anxiety had made me drift. House Minister Breteuil stood before me, his eyes glittering, almost taunting. "No doubt you are curious as to how we found Nicole d'Oliva."

"Why would I give a thought about a woman I've never met?" I responded haughtily.

Breteuil shook his head. "One of your co-conspirators was captured at the Italian border. He instructed us as to where we would find the impostor."

I could feel my heart clench as he said those words. I lowered my head, not from fear but shame, that I had taken as my name that of a betrayer. Magistrate de Marce stepped up alongside Breteuil, making no effort to hide his gloating triumph. "He has made us aware of the fraudulent notes you wrote to Cardinal Rohan in the name of the Queen."

"Furthermore," said Breteuil, "he states that

when Cardinal Rohan came to realize that the notes
were forgeries, he willingly fell in with your plans to
steal the necklace."

At this Rohan pounded the railing and began to
shout in a rage. "That is a ruinous lie! This is a
treacherous machination, Breteuil!"

I stared angrily at Breteuil. "Who is this accuser?"
I demanded. "Why are they not in attendance?"

Breteuil met my gaze with infuriating calm. "He
expressed a desire not to see you," he said flatly, and
returned to his chair.

I turned to confront the two magistrates. "During
a trial, is it not my right to confront any accuser?"

Magistrate de Marce hesitated, then nodded.
"Yes. That is correct."

"Then I demand to exercise that right, and see
who it is who shames me so!"

The Magistrates conferred with each other, then
with President d'Aligre and Breteuil. At last Magistrate de Marce turned back to me and nodded.

"You may visit him. Guards, escort her to the
Bastille. We will follow immediately. This court is
adjourned until further notice."

>❧ I HAD THOUGHT MY OWN CELL A DISMAL
place, with little light and no warmth and only a
plain deal table to hold my things. But I assure you,
it was a paradise compared to the chamber where I

was taken by the guards. The heavy oaken door needed two men to pry it open. Once it was, there was no more light within than if we stood at the threshold of a cavern. The guards indicated that I was to enter: I did so reluctantly, fearful that once inside the door would be pulled shut upon me and I too would be doomed to be forgotten in that dreadful place. The House Minister and the two magistrates stood behind with the guards, watching silently as I went inside.

The cell was tiny and rank with rotting straw. There was no window, and no furnishings of any kind. In the floor a huge iron ring was embedded, with a heavy chain twisting serpentine across the stone floor. The chain led to the shackled figure of a man lying on the floor, his back to me. Tears burned my eyes as I stepped toward him and knelt, touching his arm. He shrank from me, covering his face with his hands as I stroked his arm, murmuring gently.

"Let me see . . ."

Tenderly I moved his hands to his sides, and he turned his face to me. Even then it was a moment before I recognized him. His eyes were nearly swollen shut and shiny blue as plums, his mouth a raw gash. Beneath him the floor was clotted with blood and his breeches were stiff and black, as though they had been badly dyed.

"Retaux," I whispered. Horror flooded me so that I could not move. "Retaux, my God."

Behind me I heard a rustling as the magistrates and Breteuil entered, then a sharp intake of breath as the House Minister looked away. My lover reached up and touched my face.

"My dear Countess." His voice was harsh and glottal. "If I'd known I would be receiving visitors, I might have done something with myself."

He attempted a broken smile, and I felt tears scoring my cheeks. "My love," I said in despair. "What have they done?"

Retaux beckoned me closer. I bent until my face was beside his, and heard his hoarse whisper. "I have it on good authority that Nicolas made it to Austria. He is beyond their reach now."

"I'm glad for it," I murmured. I remained beside him for some minutes, then stood and walked to the door. Breteuil was there, blocking my exit, but I glared at him until he moved aside. In the dank corridor I found a water bucket; I carried it back to the cell and knelt once more beside Retaux.

"They practiced humiliations upon me that I could not allow to continue," he said. A fit of coughing overcame him. "Perhaps a man less vain than myself would not have relented."

Gently I raised his head and trickled water from my cupped palm into his ruined mouth. "Everyone gives in at the last," I said.

"You wouldn't have." Tears brimmed in his eyes; when they coursed down his face they were bright with blood. "Forgive me, Jeanne. Forgive me or I cannot live with myself."

I cradled him as he began to shake with convulsive sobs. After a moment I nestled my face against his, and whispered, "I love you, Retaux. That should have been enough."

And I held him as long as I could, knowing it would be the last time I would ever do so.

I WAS NOT ESCORTED BACK TO THE COURT that day, but to my cell. Rosalie had been removed to her own quarters nearby; I could hear her praying and weeping, but when I tried to speak to her, to offer her some comfort, the guards silenced me. When night fell I was so exhausted that I thought I might, at last, sleep; but then new sounds of torment echoed through the corridors: Nicole d'Oliva was in labor. Her screams were so heartrending that even I found it in my heart to consider forgiveness; but after many hours another sound broke the night, and I knew that her child was born. A boy, I could hear the midwife say. His cries joined with the wailing of the wind outside and the distant groans and imprecations of prisoners and the drunken laughter of the guards—the terrible night music of the Bastille.

Snow had begun to fall when a jailer came to my

cell. I turned from where I stood before the barred window, watching the sad beauty of flakes whirling endlessly in the darkness. The man beckoned me, waiting while I got a woolen shawl and wrapped it around my shoulders.

"Where are you taking me?" I was so frightened I could barely form the words. The jailer only shook his head.

"Follow me. You are not to speak . . ."

He took me to the small enclosed courtyard where prisoners were allowed to exercise. It was drifted high with snow, the lone chestnut tree in its center leafless and grim as a gallows. I shivered, clutching my shawl around me, wondering if my punishment was to be left here alone to freeze. But after several minutes another figure stepped into the courtyard, warmly bundled in a thick coat and fur hat.

"House Minister," I said with more bravery than I felt. "Your presence here must mean that the tally is close."

Breteuil fastidiously shook the snow from his arm, then looked at me quizzically. "The tally?"

I moved closer to him, turning my back to the wind. "Those members of Parliament bribed by you, as opposed to those bribed by Rohan."

He smiled slightly as I went on. "And there must be another contingent, made up of those you fear. Those who are beyond threats or cajolery."

Without warning his hand shot out and seized

my chin. He yanked me toward him roughly, and spat, "Before the sentences are rendered you will be given a chance to sign a confession. This confession will implicate Cardinal Rohan in a clear manner."

He released me. I shrank from him, rubbing my bruised chin, then said defiantly, "I will not."

From behind me a soft voice spoke. "That would seem to me your only chance of salvation."

I turned. In a corner of the courtyard, the Queen stepped from the shadows. She wore a simple wool cloak, no doubt to disguise her person. Her hands were hidden in a sable muff. She approached me slowly and I watched, fascinated, marveling that the Queen of all France would be here with me in a prison courtyard. Beside me Breteuil bowed, his stern look commanding me to do the same. I curtsied, but my eyes remained fixed on those of the woman before me. And I could not help but smile, to think of meeting Her Majesty thus, not in the lush gardens or halls of Versailles but here, at midnight in a snow-blown courtyard surrounded by misery and betrayal and despair.

Antoinette stopped a few feet from me. Her blue eyes regarded me coolly as she spoke. "You have an engaging smile, Countess. Though now seems a curious time to make use of it."

"I was just thinking how strange it is, Your Majesty. Of all the times I have sought you out, in the end it is you who complete the effort."

Antoinette's gaze grew hard. "I merely felt compelled to look upon the architect of such chaos."

My expression remained calm in the face of this accusation. The Queen sniffed and added disdainfully, "It must be you. Rohan is not clever enough."

"That is for Parliament to say."

For a minute Antoinette was silent. Then, shaking her head, she said, "Countess, you of all people know that I had nothing to do with this scandal."

I stared at her boldly. "Then why are the citizens so ready to believe that you did?"

Behind me Breteuil gasped. "Mind who it is you address, madame!" he cried.

"Let her speak freely." Antoinette looked at me with unfeigned interest. "We may never have another chance to understand one another. Countess?"

My words came out in a rush. "Fire does not burn unless there is tinder, Your Majesty. Likewise, excess does not fade in the minds of people, unless there is kindness to balance it."

"It makes little difference what I do in the eyes of the people!" I was taken aback by the vehemence in Antoinette's tone. "If I laugh too loudly, I am a flirt. If I chide a servant, I am an ogre. If I love my children and show them extravagances, I am draining the treasury.

"I ask you, Countess," she said, gazing at me beseechingly. "As Queen, why am I not also allowed to be human?"

I shook my head. "If it is sympathy Your Majesty

seeks, you will find it in short supply here at the Bastille."

This was more than Breteuil could bear. He lunged at me, his hand raised to strike.

"Stay where you are, Breteuil!"

At the Queen's command he halted. Reluctantly he lowered his arm. Antoinette stared at me angrily, fury glimmering in her pale blue eyes. "Countess! You have damaged my reputation and I mean to know why! Speak the truth for once, Countess. What disservice have I ever done to the likes of you?"

"You ignored me. To offer a word of advice would have cost you but a few spent breaths. But it would have meant the world to me. No doubt if you had done so, I would have traveled a different path."

Antoinette lifted her head to the falling snow. After a moment she sighed. "What's done is done. But now you must consider the broader consequences of this matter. If you weaken the monarchy, Countess, you weaken the entire nation."

I straightened and stood as proudly as I could in that dark and frigid courtyard, and said, "Your Majesty, you weakened yourselves long before a diamond necklace became the issue."

For a long time Antoinette held my gaze. Finally she said, "I've seen what I came to see." She turned and began walking away.

I had had my own trifling victory. And yet,

watching that spare, elegant figure pacing alone through the snow, a twinge of something like sorrow, and regret, and understanding shot through me. I hesitated, then called out.

"Your Majesty."

She stopped and looked at me.

"I did not set out to harm you," I said.

I thought that perhaps she might speak to me again. A full minute passed, during which we stared at each other, and I could see from the depth of feeling in her lovely eyes that yes, she understood me as well. With a slight nod she turned from me for the last time and left the courtyard. Before she reached the shelter of the building, Breteuil gave me a threatening look and hurried after her. I was left alone in the snow and the darkness.

Chapter

THIRTY-EIGHT

✦

The next morning dawned cold and gray as a knife. Overnight the snow had turned to freezing rain, making the roads dangerous and the sidewalks nearly impassable. But this did not keep the crowds from gathering outside the Palais de Justice: when my carriage arrived from the Bastille I saw a throng already huddling there beneath ragged makeshift canopies of linen. Some of them held disintegrating copies of the most recent broadsheets, with caricatures of myself and Rohan and the Queen engaged in more lewd activities than even the Cardinal could imagine. Despite the bad weather, there was a disturbing sense of anticipation in the air; I felt it as I walked, very carefully, up the palace steps, for once grateful to have the guard's hand closed tight upon my arm.

Inside I took my place before the members of Parliament. I was the last of the accused to arrive: Rohan, Cagliostro, my beloved Retaux, and Nicole d'Oliva all stood in an uneven line behind the railing. A midwife still attended Nicole, holding her infant son and clucking softly as we waited; on a bench near the back of the room Abel Duphot sat anxiously, hands tightly clasped in his lap. On the dais President d'Aligre sat, sorting through sheaves of paper and parchment. Some minutes passed while he finished tending these. I stared as long as possible at poor Retaux, wishing I could take his bruised hands, or smooth the grim lines of hopelessness from his face. Once I dared a smile, but he only met my eyes with such cold despair that I had to look away to keep from panic. After that I reserved my gaze for the floor beneath my feet, stained dark from melting slush.

Nicole passed the time by making eye contact with each Parliamentarian, until she saw someone she recognized. With a broad smile she waved her handkerchief at him. He blushed, and the other men sniggered and nudged each other.

This seemed to spur President d'Aligre. With a frown he sat up in his high-backed chair, and raised a hand for silence. The room immediately grew as still as a country boneyard. The President cleared his throat, looked around at the expectant faces of Parliament, and began.

"As concerns the charges of theft and conspiracy, the decisions rendered by this body of judges are to be carried out this day without hesitation or appeal.

"Nicole Leguay d'Oliva. You are hereby acquitted on the grounds of insufficient evidence. The acquittal is to be accompanied by a reprimand from the court, for impersonation of a sovereign."

Nicole's guileless blue eyes widened. "It means innocent, yes?"

D'Aligre nodded. "Yes."

Nicole turned and took her baby from the midwife, cuddling him against her breast, then shot a delighted, complicit smile at the judges. D'Aligre continued.

"Count Cagliostro, you are hereby acquitted of all charges without reprimand. You are to be considered exonerated by this body of judges."

For a fraction of a second, I witnessed Cagliostro's shoulders sag with relief. Then he composed himself, smiling, and made a polished bow to the assembly. "A wise and just decision," he declared.

"Marc Antoine Retaux de Vilette." Retaux stiffened, his blackened eyes staring at the floor. "You have been found guilty. You are hereby condemned to banishment for life from the Kingdom of France. All of your properties and goods are to be forfeited to the King."

A small cry escaped me then. Retaux said nothing, but when two guards stepped forward to take his arms, he pulled away and lunged toward me. I reached for his hand, and in that instant saw all I had lost: so much more than my home, my child-hood, even my sister.

"Retaux," I whispered; but with muttered oaths the guards dragged him out of the chamber and to a waiting tumbrel. I never saw him again.

On the dais, President d'Aligre set aside Retaux's pronouncement and turned to the next page of his ledger. I could see the men of Parliament leaning forward on their benches, as though straining to read what he had written. An agonizing minute passed while the President found his place. Then, "Cardinal Louis de Rohan, Grand Almoner of France and Blood Prince of the House of Rohan . . ." D'Aligre's booming voice echoed through the chamber. "This body of judges acquits you on all charges without reprimand."

My ears were deafened by the cheers of those judges who had supported Rohan. The Cardinal raised his eyes heavenward, his hands joined as though in prayer. Suddenly his legs seemed to fail him, and he tottered forward. With a low cry Abel Duphot rushed to his side and led him to a chair.

"Your Eminence!" he said. "Thank God, you will recover from this scandal—"

I looked around the room, stunned by the deci-sion, and saw from his stricken expression that House Minister Breteuil, at least, felt much as I did. All around the chamber the members of Parliament buzzed with excitement over the verdict. President d'Aligre raised his hand, vainly summoning silence. When after five minutes the noise had not subsided, he directed the guards to pound the handles of their pikes on the floor.

The gallery abruptly grew still. Every gaze burned upon me, and I closed my eyes, waiting to hear my fate.

"Jeanne de La Motte-Valois. Your verdict has been rendered—but it will not be read here at this time." My eyes shot open and I stared at him in disbelief. "You are to be detained here, in the Conciergerie, until informed otherwise."

Before another babble of talk could overtake the room, I raced past the railing toward the President. "I wish to know why my verdict is withheld! Answer me, Messieurs!" I said wildly, turning to the Parliament. "I have that right!"

President d'Aligre turned his back to me. As I struggled to reach him guards seized my arms and began to lead me toward the side chamber. I fought them shouting, "This is an outrage! Tell me now! Why can't I know? Tell me!"

But I was no match for the guards. As they dragged me from the dais I looked back at d'Aligre. "No, please," I begged. "Do not do this. Uphold your office, Monsieur. Tell me what is to happen to me. *I must know.*"

Even as they pulled me through the doors I kept crying out, pleading with him; but President d'Aligre refused to turn and meet my eyes.

Chapter

THIRTY-NINE

F ar removed as he was from the common people, they had clearly taken the Cardinal's side over Antoinette's. That night a carnival atmosphere prevailed over the House of Rohan, as the Cardinal's supporters gathered below his balcony. Inside, Abel Duphot helped dress him with that luxury earned by fear, in his finest robes, while servants brought trays of fruit and cheeses for his delectation.

"Your Eminence." Abel Duphot stepped back, admiring his work: the Cardinal stood resplendent before the looking glass. "I think perhaps it is time now for you to greet your supporters."

He inclined his head toward the window. The Cardinal nodded, and walked out onto the balcony.

"Long live the Cardinal!" Cheers erupted from below; Rohan stared down, amazed and touched. Hundreds of people had braved the cold to stand there in the snow, waving torches and handmade banners with the Rohan coat of arms painted on it.

"Long live Parliament!"

"Long live the House of Rohan!"

"Justice is done!"

That night, Cardinal Rohan found himself a national hero. He remained outside for almost an hour, with Abel Duphot at his side to wipe away the occasional tear. When at last he retired it was near midnight, and he fell asleep with the sound of his name still being echoed throughout the château.

WHEN NEWS OF THE VERDICTS REACHED Versailles that evening, a smothering despair settled over the Royal House. Louis, the children, and several of the more loyal Palace servants gathered outside the Queen's bedchamber. Behind the gilt-edged door, agonized wails rent the night. The children whimpered, and Louis hugged his son close.

Inside, Madame Campan sat on the bed, rocking the distraught Antoinette in her arms. "Do not think this way," she murmured. "Please—"

The Queen's dressing gown was torn and she wore no wig: her own hair hung disheveled past her shoulders. "They vindicate Rohan to cause me anguish!" she cried. "It is an affront to my womanhood!"

"Do not do this to yourself, Your Majesty. I beg you!"

Antoinette pushed her away and stumbled to her feet. "Parliament has told the world they do not believe my character is free of scandal! They have chosen to absolve a common whore of sin, but not their Queen!"

She lurched against a table holding clocks and crystal. With a muffled scream she sent it crashing to the floor, then weeping lowered herself onto a settee near the window. Her face was swollen with tears; when she looked up into an oval looking glass it cast back the reflection of a grotesque, tormented creature, red-faced and haglike. "I will give them what they want," she cried. "I will live here quietly, in my disgrace. It's what they've always wanted!"

She picked up a porcelain miniature and threw it at the looking glass. The mirror shattered into a thousand glittering fragments. The Queen shook her head, staring dully at the broken shards covering the floor, and pronounced, "My happy years have ended on this day."

Chapter

FORTY

I spent the next three weeks in the Conciergerie of the Palais de Justice. The Concierge and his wife were kind to me. For the first few days I did not speak or even move at all; only lay upon the lumpy mattress stuffed with straw which was my bed and tried to drown out the exultant sounds of which still resounded from outside.

"Viva la France!"

"Vive le Cardinal de Rohan!"

"Justice! We have Justice!"

"Death to the Monarchy! Death to the King's whore!"

Still the Concierge's wife would each day bring me food, the simple fare which they themselves ate, bread and cheese and dried apples, and strong Rhone wine to wash it down. After I began to eat once more she would sit with me sometimes, and I would question her about what was going on outside.

"Oh, it goes badly for the King and Queen," she said, shaking her head as she nibbled on a rind of cheese. "She has spent all the people's money: we starve while she entertains her friends, and now there is talk of revolution. Already there are riots here in Paris."

"And my sentence? Is there any news from the President as to when I shall be freed?"

Again she shook her head. "This I do not know, Countess. But be grateful, for the moment, that you are somewhere safe and warm and protected. It goes badly these days for the aristocracy, and for anyone who is associated with them."

It was the end of the third week when they came for me. Dawn was a feeble gray gleam at my window, and I was sound asleep, my head pillowed on the small bundle of clothes which was all that remained of my fortune. When the Concierge's wife shook me awake I sat bolt upright, my heart thundering in my breast.

"What is it? Is it a reprieve? Am I to go free?"

"Shh—quickly, quickly, there's no time for us to talk now. Later, Countess—"

I got up hastily, still in my nightclothes, and stumbled across the room as she waited impatiently, holding a candle-nub and looking anxiously at the door. When we left my room her husband joined us in the hall.

"This way, Countess."

"But where—"

I followed them through winding passages, until finally we came to a large wooden door. He opened it, gesturing for me to enter before him.

"Concierge," I began; then the breath froze in my throat.

I was in the Grand Chamber. The room was empty save for President d'Aligre, the Court Scribe, and two men wearing black and gray: the Executioner Sanson and his aide. I turned to see the Concierge and his wife gazing at me with pity and shame. Then Sanson and his aide grabbed me and pulled me before the President.

"No! Please, I beg you!"

My sentence had not been read with the others because of its insidious nature: it was feared the huge crowds present three weeks earlier would have rioted in an effort to free me. I marvel now that the President too was not overcome with shame, to declare my punishment.

"Jeanne de La Motte-Valois!" he cried, though there were only those few of us present. "The sentence rendered by this court of judges will now be read.

"On this day, you are to be remanded to the custody of the People's Executioner. You are to be publicly flogged with an implement of the Executioner's choosing. You are to be branded on the shoulder with the identifying mark of a thief. After a short period of recovery, you will be taken to the Salpetriere, where you will be imprisoned for the rest of your life.

"The judgment of Parliament is final. Justice has been served."

"No!"

He ignored my screams as I was dragged into the courtyard of the Palais de Justice. Citizens and reporters pressed gray faces against the iron gates, shivering in the cold. In the windows of the surrounding buildings I could see other faces, small and white, peering down at me. Despite all the secrecy, there were many, many there to witness my punishment. It was the greatest humiliation of my life.

In the center of the icy courtyard was a stanchion, shoulder-high, with a noose hanging from it. A few feet away a small blacksmith's stove glowed orange, a brand heating in its coals. I fought desperately but was no match for Sanson and his assistant, who carried me bodily to the post and looped the noose around my neck. I screamed, kicking at them; but I might have been kicking at the frozen ground itself, they were that unyielding. The aide forced me to the ground while Sanson strode behind me. I could hear the sound of a knife being drawn from a scabbard, and then the sound of my nightclothes being slashed down the back. I shrieked, trying to cover my nakedness, but worse was to come.

The executioner beat me, lashing me with a wooden rod as I rolled helplessly on the ground, screaming in pain. My blood mingled with slush and filth, staining the ground beneath the post; my hair grew matted with blood and tears. Still my misery would not end: the executioner stepped away, silent and ominous, and took the heated branding iron from its trough of glowing coals. I could hear gasps and muttered prayers from those watching behind the gate.

"Dear God, she is to be branded!"

Somehow I found the strength then to stagger to my feet, and slip the rope from my neck. I lurched across the courtyard, but Sanson grabbed me. His aide rushed to my other side, pulling back the shreds of my nightgown to expose my shoulder. I twisted my head, biting at his wrist as Sanson brought the brand down; but my sudden motion threw him slightly off balance. The brand pressed against my right breast instead of my shoulder, searing a blood-red letter V, for *voleuse* —

Thief.

The anguish was indescribable. I wailed, swaying numbly as before me the faces of onlookers blurred into one vast mass of flesh and eyes. The last thing I can recall before I sank to the ground, unconscious, was a taunting voice crying out gleefully.

"At last, she's got her coat of arms . . ."

⤚ THOUGH MYRIAD RUMORS SWEPT THE COUN-try as to my eventual fate, the truth was rather common, and sad. I was taken to the Salpetriere, a woman's prison of the most horrible conditions. There I languished in filth for nearly two years. Sometimes, from the courtyard or through a grated window, we could see the smoke of distant fires in the city. We heard rumors from outside, but had no idea of the vast changes that were taking place. It was not until I effected my escape from that dread-ful place, and arrived here, to the safety of English soil, that I learned of the Revolution and the fate of Antoinette. She who had wanted so much to be loved by her adopted countrymen was convicted of treason and executed by guillotine, by the very public she so desperately wished to understand. It seemed to me, then and now, the cruelest tragedy of all.

Still, when news of the Queen's demise fell upon my ears, it was as if, at last, a book had been gently closed within me. For Jeanne de La Motte-Valois, the Affair of the Diamond Necklace had at last come to an end. I should like to return to France someday, but I do not think that I shall fight to advance the name of Valois within the new republic. My experiences have taught me that honor does not live in a name. It comes from what others know you carry in your heart.

For now, that is enough.

The French Monarchy never regained credibility after the Necklace Affair. The trial of Cardinal Rohan, Cagliostro, and the Comtesse de La Motte-Valois was a rallying point for the Revolution that followed.

Shortly after the verdicts, Cardinal Rohan was stripped of all titles by Louis XVI. He was exiled to the Abbey of Chaise-Dieu, where piety continued to elude him for the rest of his days.

Count Cagliostro left France. He was later found guilty of sorcery during the Italian Inquisition. He proclaimed that he would live longer than the wall of his prison would remain standing. He did not.

Retaux de Vilette wrote and published his memoirs of the Necklace Affair. After the book's release, he settled down with a spinster duchess 31 years his senior. He never saw Jeanne again.

Nicolas de La Motte returned to Paris after the Revolution, where he made a living extorting money from the Rohan family *not* to write his memoirs.

Jeanne de La Motte never returned to France. She was killed in London after being thrown from a third-story window. Enemies claimed it happened during a drunken orgy. Friends said it was done by agents of the French Royal Family. The truth was never known.